All she could see ... piercing eyes and tempting mouth.

He was close enough that the scent of his cologne mixed pleasantly with the water-and-sand aroma. His body was just broad enough, just muscled enough to make her feel sheltered, protected.

"I've been thinking of something else that might elicit a pretty good feeling."

Better than what she was feeling now that he had her enfolded in his arms? She could only imagine.

But even her imagination wasn't that good.

His head descended slowly, just enough to have her catching her breath. His lips touched hers in a whisper, like the barest summer breeze. Impatient and hungry for more, she came up on her tiptoes, wrapping her arms around his neck, opening her mouth to his. Their lips touched again, soft, slow. It was hard to follow his lead, but his firm grip on her said that's the way he wanted it. She let him kiss her slowly again, just his lips. That small act stole her breath.

Books by A.C. Arthur

Kimani Romance

Love Me Like No Other
A Cinderella Affair
Guarding His Body
Second Chance, Baby
Defying Desire
Full House Seduction
Summer Heat
Sing Your Pleasure
Touch of Fate

ARTIST C. ARTHUR

was born and raised in Baltimore, Maryland, where she currently resides with her husband and three children. An active imagination and a love for reading encouraged her to begin writing in high school and she hasn't stopped since.

Determined to bring a new edge to romance, she continues to develop intriguing plots, racy characters and fresh dialogue—thus keeping readers on their toes! Visit her website at www.acarthur.net.

Touch
of Fate

A.C. Arthur

KIMANI
ROMANCE

If you don't know where you are going,
You should know where you came from.
—Gullah proverb

KIMANI PRESS™

ISBN-13: 978-0-373-86217-7

TOUCH OF FATE

Recycling programs
for this product may
not exist in your area.

Dear Reader,

Once again I find myself in another place as I tell the story of Maxwell Donovan and Deena Lakefield. Visiting Hilton Head Island was like taking a long vacation, sitting on the shore watching the waves in a picturesque town. The scenery could not have been more romantic and what better place to start a love story as emotionally satisfying as this one.

As you may remember, Max has been around since the beginning of The Donovans—*Love Me Like No Other* (Linc & Jade's story). He's the supportive and loyal cousin who gives advice sparingly but is always there through thick and thin. Now it's time Max faced the biggest secret of his life, and who better to do that with than the vivacious and spirited Deena Lakefield.

It is my hope that this story touches your heart the same way it did mine. When a different kind of hero finds his true love, I can't help but be elated. And at the end of the day as I sit on the beach watching the sun set I can lift a glass and toast to the newest love match in the Donovan family and wonder who will be next.

Happy reading!

AC

If you don't know where you are going,
You should know where you came from.
                              —Gullah Proverb

Chapter 1

June—Hilton Head, South Carolina

Sterile.

Never have children.

Weeping. So much weeping, it echoed in his mind like a broken record. He tried to focus on sleep, resting his mind and his body that had been through so much, but it was useless. Hospitals were meant for the sick, to give them time to rest and recover. But how was one supposed to do that when there were constant interruptions, like nurses coming to poke a needle in your arm or stick a thermometer in your mouth? And doctors who came bearing one bad diagnosis after another; and family members who rallied around like the support system they were meant to be, talking and soothing, praying and smiling through tears.

He hadn't rested, not since the first punch had been thrown and he'd ended up on the floor in a corner, bleeding, choking, dying. But he hadn't died, he'd lived and was now dealing with the repercussions that some would consider his fate.

A fate that had destroyed the part of his future that had meant the most to him.

With sweat pouring from his face, his heart thumping wildly in his chest, Maxwell Donovan shot straight up in his bed. Sheets twisted around his slim waist, tangling between his legs, enough to cover his nudity and restrain the wild kicking that often accompanied his nightmares.

He was wide awake now. The dream allowed for nothing else. His first inclination was to work so he'd retrieved his laptop from its case on the small desk in the corner of the room. Dragging his hands down his face he took deep breaths while waiting for the computer to boot up.

They were back. The dreams. No, the nightmares.

For months, almost a year, they'd disappeared. He'd been sleeping just fine, living even better.

Donovan Investments, Inc., the real estate investment business he'd gone into with his partner and cousin, Adam Donovan, seven years ago was thriving. In the past year they'd made over ten purchases and resales, almost tripling their profit from the year before. Sure, the country was in a recession and new home mortgages were on the downslide—even with President Obama's new home buyers tax credit—the fact still remained that people generally paid for what they wanted and begged for what they needed. Meaning, people who wanted larger homes or better-looking business offices were still in the buying market. Now, five to ten years from now would they be able to afford the decisions they'd made in the past year? Max didn't have the answer to that, nor did he spend too many nights trying to figure it out. He wasn't in the lending business.

Through their company he and Adam searched for viable properties, most often through estates and word of mouth. They refurbished the properties then sold them for a larger profit. What set them apart from the proverbial house flippers seen on television reality shows was that they didn't work in residential real estate. Office buildings, retail spaces and, now, resorts were where they concentrated their efforts.

And those efforts were paying off, he and Adam, along with their seventy-five-person staff, were making a more than comfortable living at their jobs. Business was good, so for Max that meant life was good.

Then everything in the Donovan family began to go haywire.

His generation of Donovan men, who were self-proclaimed "not the marrying type" for various reasons, were now getting hitched and starting families. His three cousins, Lincoln, Trent and Adam, had all taken the plunge. Linc and his wife, Jade, now had twin girls, while Trent and his wife of six months, Tia, had already welcomed a little boy into their family. Adam and his wife, Camille, were embarking on two exciting events—Camille's fashion design company had expanded globally and they were now in Rome where her first international show was about to take place. And, as if that weren't enough, Camille was seven months pregnant with their first child. Hence the reason

Max was here in Hilton Head, South Carolina, looking over the faltering Sandy Pines Resort.

Pulling up his email he saw the one from his mother and had to smile.

Alma Donovan was another big part of the reason he was here and not Adam. It was her connection to this particular land in Hilton Head that first alerted Max and Adam to the prospect. The land northeast of US 278, or William Hilton Parkway, nestled along Broad Creek, between the Wexford and Long Cove Plantations, had belonged to Alma's great-great-grandfather, Eustis Johnson. It was said that the money Eustis earned as a result of being one of the first black soldiers in the Union troop during the Civil War had allowed him to buy the land on Hilton Head Island, the island that once consisted almost entirely of African-Americans with deep historic roots. Hilton Head began its transformation into an almost all-white, upscale golf, tennis and shopping mecca in the late 1950s. Therefore, the land had gone from owner to owner, mostly staying within the Johnson family. It was with the passing of Alma's third cousin that it had finally fallen into Alma's name. And she wanted her son to make something of their legacy, something she and the rest of the Johnsons could be proud of.

So far, Max wasn't impressed with what was being called the Sandy Pines Resort. He'd only been here two days but his first impression was that the previous owner had tried to compete with the existing gated communities around Hilton Head and failed dismally. Probably because of money.

Nina, Max's assistant at his office back in Las Vegas, had done some research prior to his departure and emailed him all the information on the island he needed. Bypassing his mother's email, he pulled up Nina's and opened some of the files she'd sent. Hilton Head's transformation was due partly to money—that wasn't surprising. Developers with high ideas and deep pockets had invaded the all-but-forgotten island, getting a return on their investment that probably surpassed their wildest dreams.

The question for Max was did Donovan Investments repeat what had been working for so long on this prosperous island? Or should they do what they always did—break all the rules to come out on top?

That put him back to the meeting he had just before leaving Vegas. The one that Alma called with him and Adam.

"I want you boys to do this right," she'd said the moment they both sat down at the conference table in their office.

She'd worn a business suit, which was usually what his mother wore; whether it be pants or a skirt, she was always ready for business. You'd never guess she'd been a housewife most of her fifty-five years. She had earned a BA in Business a year before marrying Everette Donovan. But since Everette was a third partner, along with two of his brothers, in this generation of the Donovan oil legacy, there had been no need for Alma to take her degree further. Or at least that's what Everette first thought. After settling into marriage and having two sons, Max and Benjamin, separated by two years, Alma began to work a little here and there at home. Her work consisted mainly of helping Everette with his business dealings. After Max and Ben finished college and moved out of their family home in Nevada she'd teamed up with her sister-in-law, Beverly Donovan, making sure the Donovan name still had clout in the area of philanthropy. Between the two of them they had several charities going, along with their own foundation for women. And now, so it seemed, another pet project for Alma.

"You're good at what you do, there's no doubt about that or I wouldn't trust this to you. But I want you to know exactly what I envision before you go any further."

Adam tossed Max a questioning look that Max knew better than to return. When his mother was about business there was no playing involved. Adam, for whatever reason, acted like he'd forgotten that.

"So tell us about this project, Mom," he'd said in his most professional voice, pulling out his legal pad and pen, prepared to take notes. That's what he would have done at any other meeting, only this wasn't any other meeting. Very rarely did he and Adam have clients come to them with a property they wanted to refurbish and keep. So he was all ears to his mother's plan. At least for the moment.

"You've been to the island before, Max. Your father and I took you and Ben a couple of times when you were younger. That's when Aunt Jocenda had the place. Then her crazy twin sister got it after Jocenda died in that plane crash. Jessa was always a bit touched but her parents never wanted to admit it."

"So there was a crazy woman running this…what? A bed-and-breakfast on Hilton Head Island?" Adam questioned. "That sounds like a plot point in a horror novel." He chuckled.

"You're still the most playful of Beverly's boys,"

Alma said with a half grin. "I thought when Camille married you, you'd settle it down a little. I guess she hasn't gotten that far yet."

Adam was already shaking his head. "Camille loves to laugh. I like to oblige her when I can. But seriously, Aunt Alma, what is it you think we can do with this place? And why us? If you already own the property you could just hire contractors to refurbish the place for you. Then you could hire staff to run it, make an income off it for yourself. You don't really need to get us involved." He shrugged.

"Oh, but I do," she said, pulling out a folder full of old photos. "This is what the house looked like when I was a little girl."

Adam took a few pictures then slid some to Max. He looked down at what struck him as a house right out of history. Big, palatial, like an old Southern plantation. Wraparound porch, miles of grass, big magnolia trees lining the walkway. He was instantly taken back to a time and place before he was born, when African Americans didn't have the right to read, much less own a house of this magnitude.

"And you say your great-great-grandfather, Eustis, owned this house and this land. Was this documented?" he asked.

"Of course it was documented, Maxwell. Don't act like we're thieves or liars. Because we're not. I come from much more dignified stock than that."

Justly scorned, Max nodded. "Okay, so the land is legally yours now. Does the house still look like this?"

"Somewhat, but not really. Jessa had the idea that she could change the house into a resort like the other big ones down in Hilton Head now, but she failed. Just like she failed in everything else she did."

"Because she didn't have enough money," Adam guessed.

"That and because she didn't have a lick of sense. You can't run a resort if half the occupants are no-good drunks out to use you for the little bit you have. Jessa was always being used. I suspect because everybody could see she didn't have it all going on upstairs," Alma said, tapping a finger against her temple. "Anyway, that's all done. The good Lord saw fit to carry Jessa on home with the rest of her family. Now, it's in my hands and I'm so thankful that I've been blessed enough in my lifetime to be able to do it right."

"You want to keep it as a resort?" Max asked, thinking he could see where his mother was going with this.

"That's right." Alma nodded. "But I want it to look like this again," she said, pointing to the pictures in front of them.

"There's acres and acres of land here, Aunt Alma. Do you want to build on some additions? Increase the number of guests that can be accommodated?"

"No, I want it to remain exactly the same size. I think it's about ten rooms as it stands now, upstairs and down, not including living quarters for the staff."

"The staff doesn't have to live there. They can live elsewhere on the island, increasing the rooms to be rented out," Max said but Alma was already shaking her head.

"No, I want it like it was when I used to go as a little girl. There was always somebody in that big house. People who took care of it all the time, faces I'd seen so much I thought they were related as well. They lived there so it made it all the more important to take good care of the space. And it was a home away from home. Not a hotel. Everybody felt comfortable there. We had breakfasts together in the big dining room, lunch usually out on the porch. Dinner back in the dining room. It was all timed and respected. The land was always well tended. Nice green grass, bright white magnolias and lots and lots of flowers in the gardens around back. The children had space to play while the grown-ups tended to their business. It was like a haven away from the rest of the world. That's what I want to give vacationers. Not golf and yachting or expensive shops and boutiques. I want to give them some old Southern comfort."

Max sighed as he remembered the conversation. Looking around the room at the peeling paint and ragged wood planked floors he rubbed his neck. Bringing his mother's dream into this reality was going to be tough. But they could do it. She believed in him and Adam—in the business they had built. So much so she'd given them free reign and a limitless budget to get the project done.

So Max was determined to do just that. No matter how much his nightmares haunted him.

She'd messed up again.

That's what her family would say.

Deena Lasharon Lakefield propped her feet onto the balcony railing and sat back in her chair. The warm South Carolina air massaged her skin as she closed her eyes, ticking off the events of the past week.

Reviews for her first romance novel, *Until Tomorrow,* were flooding in and were all good. She was a success, or at least her story was with the readers. Financially, her editor had advised she'd have to wait a couple months to see how sales went. But Deena was optimistic, always.

She deserved a vacation. Her older sister, Monica, had dutifully made the observation that Deena's entire life was a vacation. Even more according to duty, Deena ignored her.

In Monica's eyes, Deena was the immature sister, the careless and carefree one. So there was no surprise that every opportunity she had Monica was reprimanding her for something. But even if Deena tried to be more like her older sister—which she definitely did not because the world didn't need another coldhearted workaholic woman mad at the entire male species— it just wouldn't work. Deena wasn't cut out to be a businesswoman. Her talent was to create.

As for her other sister, Karena, Deena admired her strength and her latest decision to cut down on some of her work hours and enjoy life. That could be due to the very handsome Sam Desdune, who'd worn Karena and her misguided ideas about relationships down.

In the supermarket she'd seen a brochure tacked onto the community board. She'd taken it down because she loved the scene of an old Southern plantation boasting sandy beaches, cool water and relaxation from the moment she stepped onto the grounds. It had taken her another hour to get home and book her room. The next day she was packed and heading to the airport.

Now she was here, sitting on the porch and for all intents and purposes enjoying the Southern air and relaxing.

It was only when she opened her eyes to see the poor conditions of her room and the sad state of the grounds at Sandy Pines Resort that she began to rethink her decision in coming here.

It wasn't so rundown that she couldn't stay. Truth be told, the place had potential. It just didn't look well maintained. But her sheets were clean, the food was good and there was a pool that she could use twenty-four hours a day. There weren't many guests so she had plenty of peace and quiet to work on her next book. All in all, Deena would say it was working out well. Despite the discrepancies in the brochure and what Sandy Pines actually was.

To take her mind off the resort and her sisters, Deena decided to run herself a bath. Afterward, she lay in the king-size bed staring up at the ceiling, sleep successfully evading her. After about an hour of this she'd sighed and climbed out of the bed. Either she could work until she fell asleep or she could go for a swim. She decided to do both, in a roundabout way.

Plotting the great romantic love affair was a hell of a lot easier than experiencing one of her own, she thought as she padded down the wrought iron stairs on the back side of the big house. That's why she wrote fantastic love stories and took her own love life for what it was—good for the moment. Did she want the same happily ever after she wrote about? Of course she did, but she wasn't about to spend every waking moment searching for it.

Dropping her towel and room key onto one of the lounge chairs she stepped out of her shoes. It was a quiet night, the sky above was dark, yet calm and welcoming. The air was balmy with a slight breeze as she shrugged out of her robe and walked toward the water. Monica would put a toe in to test the temperature. Karena would probably sit on the side with her feet fully submerged first until she felt comfortable. Deena just jumped in.

That's how she did most things in her life. Made a decision and went for it. Some would call that impulsive. Her father called it irresponsible. Deena figured there was no other way to be and so far it was working just fine.

The water had a slight chill to it, but it didn't bother her as she swam from one end to the other. It was refreshing, cutting through the water as sleek as a fish, her mother would say. Each stroke had her mind emptying of where she was, or any of the other issues that plagued her life. All she could think about now was Joanna, the heroine in her new book.

Joanna was looking for love. Not desperately looking, but hoping it would come sooner rather than later. She was twenty-eight, the same age as Deena, and had never really been in love. Of course, Joanna had boyfriends and fell in lust a couple of times but she was certain that love had never resided in her heart for a man.

They say new authors write what they know. This was not the case for Deena. She could write about falling in love, write about lasting and satisfying relationships, but had yet to find one of her own. There was irony in that somewhere, only she didn't see it right now.

Instead she envisioned the perfect man for Joanna.

Tall, surpassing six feet. Good looking was a given, drop-dead gorgeous an added bonus. More importantly, he had to be compassionate and love life as much as Joanna did. He had to appreciate and support her or their life together would never work. Success and money didn't matter that much to Deena, much to her father's consternation. But this was a romance novel so he'd have a steady job and be a basically good guy.

With each stroke Deena thought more and more about creating Joanna's hero, so much so that she had to pause…was she thinking about the perfect man for Joanna or the perfect man for herself?

Max's mind was on a snack. As he was on the steps that creaked when you walked down, inhaling the stuffy humid air walking through the house, in his head he ticked off an endless list of changes as he moved into the large kitchen and flicked on the light.

He didn't expect what he saw.

A butterfly, full-colored wings and lavish detail, drawn on skin the exact color of a milk chocolate bar.

On impulse his body tightened with arousal.

But when she turned around, smiled and said, "Hello," all the air deflated from his lungs, his mouth momentarily going dry.

"Hello," he finally managed when he realized he was standing like a mute.

"I was just getting a glass of water," she said then turned back to the cupboard where she was reaching for a glass.

They were on the highest shelf and he thought, *thank you, Lord,* as the hip-riding shorts she wore over her bathing suit bottom didn't reach upward with the rest of her body. The butterfly he'd first noticed, which was strategically located just above her buttocks, was again noticeable.

He could hear his cousin Trent saying now, "There's nothing hotter than a tramp stamp." That's what tattoos in this particular location on a female were called. And right about now, no matter how rare an occasion it was that he actually agreed with Trent, Max felt his cousin's words were the honest truth.

Not only was this tattoo hot, but the tight little body it was attached to was pretty damn spectacular as well. She wasn't tall, maybe five feet four inches. But she was shaped like a woman definitely familiar with a gym. He noted her toned legs and well-defined arms. Her bottom was tight and round and his mouth was watering.

Clearing his throat, Max reminded himself that he was thirty-five years old, not sixteen.

"It's late," he said finally.

She was turning on the faucet, sticking the glass she'd retrieved from the cabinet beneath it. Turning back to face him, she folded one arm over flat abs left bare by the bikini top she wore. Lifting the glass to her mouth she gave him a quizzical look. "I know. Couldn't sleep. Since you're standing down here with me at this late hour I have to conclude that you can't either."

"True," he responded with a nod. "How long have you been here? At the resort I mean, not in the kitchen?"

She smiled and Max thought maybe the sun was coming out early.

"Just a couple of days. I'm Deena Lakefield," she said offering her free hand to him.

Closing the distance between them, he took her extended hand. *Petite* would seem like the right word for her. Still, he had an idea there was much more to her than her slight size.

"Max Donovan. I've been here a couple days, too. Wonder why we haven't met before now."

She shrugged. "I've been working a lot from my room."

"What type of work do you do?"

She paused, like she was considering her answer, then with a tilt of her head said, "I'm a writer."

"Really?" He would have placed her in media or something where she could talk and smile. It seemed she liked to do both. He liked to see and hear her do both. "What do you write?"

Her brown eyes brightened, her grin going from cordially nice to sensually soft. "Romance," she said, her voice lowering slightly. "Know anything about that subject, Max Donovan?"

Chapter 2

Was she flirting with him?

Of course she was. He was, hands down, the finest man she'd ever seen. And because she'd gotten into boys early—at around ten was when she had started noticing the opposite sex—she'd seen her fair share of good-looking men.

But this man was like a walking god. All right, that was probably cliché, she'd blame that on the romance writer's mind. Still, she couldn't argue the facts.

He was tall—damn, she loved tall men—over six feet, like a good couple of inches above it, she concluded. His skin was the color of melted caramel, his eyes some dreamy toss-up between green and gray. It was hard to tell in this kitchen with the not-so-great lighting. He was muscled and sculpted and just basically existing as if he were meant to be painted, put in a frame and thoroughly enjoyed. His hair was great, she surmised immediately. Thick, a sandy-brown color and long. Not down his back long, but not close-cropped either. Actually, it looked as if he may have at one point had dreads or twists, because the two- to three-inch length looked wavy and soft. That was really the clincher for her since her own hair was worn in shoulder-length twists. She loved natural styles and applauded men for stepping outside the box and wearing their hair differently as well.

She wanted to lick him, like a caramel lollipop. That made her sound like a slut with a sweet tooth.

Yet, it was so true.

Standing here in this old-fashioned kitchen with its linoleum floor and Formica countertops with the moonlight spilling through the windows was the perfect prelude to hot summer sex.

And her imagination was on total overload.

"You write romance novels? Hmm, wouldn't have pegged you for the fairy-tale type."

He was talking.

Stop ogling him and talk maturely, she warned herself.

"Why? What's wrong with fairy tales?"

"Reality's better," he said and she knew he was being honest. She liked that in a man.

"A fairy tale can happen in real life. It's all about the imagination. Prince Charming can come in many forms, a millionaire businessman, a talented NBA player, a suit-and-tie corporate type, the cable guy," she said, ticking off her answers with her fingers.

He smiled. His eyes changed when he did, becoming a little lighter, she thought.

"Come on, would you really consider the cable guy a Prince Charming?"

"If he provided the heroine with everything she needed or desired, yes. It's not about the wrapping, it's what's beneath that makes the package worth while."

There, chew on that a minute, Mr. Nonbeliever.

He shrugged. "Okay, I guess you can rationalize your opinion. So what brings you here? Are you from South Carolina?"

"No."

"I didn't think so. No Southern accent."

"I'm from New York. My family runs an art gallery there." She wasn't sure why she'd told him this. She never used her family background to impress men. Ever. Was she trying to impress him?

"What do you do, Max?" she asked, loving the way his name rolled off her tongue.

"I'm in real estate," he responded. Then, with a nod of his head, he signaled that they should have a seat at the big table across the room.

The chairs were wooden, as was most of the furniture here. But she liked the kitchen, with its big windows and open floor plan. Cabinets lined the better part of two walls, with windows decorated with eyelet curtains at equal intervals. The floor was bright white with little blue flowers, an old design but it worked in here. Pulling out a chair, she almost smiled at the heavy feel against her hands. Old furniture, antiques, had that feel. Weathered. Used. Loved. She liked it, so she sat down.

"That's a vague answer. What do you do in real estate? Buy? Sell?"

He sat in the chair right next to hers, so close she caught a whiff of what would be his cologne, a little muted because he would have put it on early this morning, after his shower maybe. Still, the scent seemed to match what she'd seen of him. Confident. Intriguing.

"Both."

"Cryptic again. You don't like talking about yourself much, huh?"

He shrugged. "I just think there are more interesting things to talk about."

"Okay, well let's talk about the company you work for, what do they do?"

He smiled and she smiled back.

"Persistent. I like that."

His words sent little shivers dancing down her spine.

"My cousin and I are partners in a company that purchases properties, refurbishes and resells them."

"Oh, you're house flippers. I've seen them on television."

His quick frown was unmistakable. "We're not house flippers. We buy properties such as large estates, office buildings, resorts. We're a much higher class than those you see on television."

Because he seemed a bit bothered by her assessment of his business, Deena pushed on. She couldn't help it, it was just her way. "You're into the 'class' thing? Like you're better than them because you don't buy houses that everyday people would want? What class are your clients? Better yet, what class am I?"

He straightened in his chair, those intriguing eyes keeping her still, frozen in his gaze.

"First, that's not what I meant. I do not abide by any class system. I was referring to the level of real estate work I do in comparison. Second, I never judge people by their circumstances. And third, I like your tattoo."

Deena opened her mouth, fully prepared to blast his response, but then she snapped it shut. "Okay," she said finally, clearing her throat. "Ah, thanks."

He'd seen her tattoo. When? Probably when he'd first come into the kitchen because she knew she'd been alone at the pool. She shifted in her chair and tried to keep her gaze steady with his. But she had to admit, his compliment had thrown her off.

"Do you like butterflies?" he asked, his voice suddenly somber.

"Butterflies and moonlit walks."

He lifted a brow. "Are you asking me to walk with you under the moonlight?"

She stared at him a second longer, thought about what he'd asked and what she wanted. He was fine, but he was also sure of himself. Sure that he could have anything and anyone he wanted. Of course, this was her quick assessment of him and she could certainly be wrong. But for right now it was what she thought, and so, she needed to react accordingly. "No, I don't think so," she replied. "I think I've had enough for tonight."

Standing, she extended her hand. "It was a pleasure meeting you, Mr. Donovan."

Max, still in awe of her quick wit and spirited personality, not to mention her pretty face and sexy tattoo, stood, taking her offered hand. Before he could examine the action, he was lifting her hand to his lips and placing a tender kiss on its back. "The pleasure was all mine, Ms. Lakefield," he said.

Slipping her hand easily out of his grip, she said simply, "Good night."

Yes, Max thought when she'd left him alone in the

kitchen. This had turned out to be a good night. And if he had his way it would end up being a very good trip.

New York

"She's where?" Monica Lakefield slammed her briefcase onto her desk before pulling out her chair and taking a seat.

"Hilton Head, South Carolina," Karena replied in a tone that was too nonchalant for her.

"What's she doing there?"

"Probably writing her next book."

"Book? Are you serious? When is she going to find a job?"

Karena sighed. "Writing is her job, Monica. Her book's in the stores in case you didn't know."

"I know about the book. I've ordered a couple hundred of them in the past week. But really," she said, her coral-painted nails moving swiftly over the keyboard, "is she making this a full-time permanent thing?"

"Yes. I think she is. Actually, I think she should. She's good, Monica. You should read one of those hundreds of books you bought. This might be what she really needs to do."

"She really needs a steady income and a pension plan." Monica sighed. Why was she the only person in her family who thought along the lines of responsibility? Well, there was her father, Paul Lakefield, but he was more like a dictator in Monica's book. She, on the other hand, was just being practical.

"Deena will be fine. She has her trust fund that she hasn't touched. And besides, Deena's always done whatever was necessary to take care of herself. She doesn't ask us for anything."

"You're right," Monica agreed. Her youngest sister never asked her for help. Truth be told, Monica was a little hurt by that fact. But she'd never let anybody else know that.

"Well, does she at least have an agent or an attorney to make sure she's not signing her soul away on one of those publishing contracts?"

"Last time I talked to her she was interviewing a couple of prospects. Don't know if she's actually signed with one yet, but it's one of her priorities."

Monica chuckled.

Karena looked at her in a funny way.

"What?"

"Nothing. I just can't remember the last time I heard you laugh."

"Well, I'm not the one shacking up with the handsome detective so maybe I don't have anything to laugh about. But you've got to admit, Deena with priorities is funny."

Karena smiled. "At one time you would have been right but I think she's changing."

Karena had reached into her own briefcase, no doubt to pull out the sales report they were meeting to go over. That was to signal the end of the discussion on Deena.

Monica still wasn't certain she liked the idea of her sister being so far away by herself but recognized there wasn't a whole lot she could do about it at the moment. Maybe Deena was changing, maybe she could handle things on her own. No, her little sister was still naive to the world and all its pitfalls. For that reason she vowed to keep a close eye on her, to make sure that nothing or anyone would ever hurt Deena, the way she'd been hurt.

She'd done something different with her hair today. The shoulder-length locks had been pulled up in the front, twisted into some kind of knot, a red flower adding a splash of color. The flower matched a long flowing skirt of red and white and a skimpy red halter top that showed more skin than was probably legal. On her feet were a combination of sassy straps and sexy heels.

Max was totally undone.

He'd thought about her all through the night—or the remaining hours after he'd found himself a snack in the kitchen. Laying in his bed while an almost-cool breeze seeped into his room, making the thin gauze curtains dance mysteriously, all he could see was her smiling face. There was something bright and fresh about Miss Deena Lakefield that Max hadn't encountered in a very long time.

In the circles he and his cousins ran in back in Vegas, women came in one of two categories: fast and ready to seduce, those were the ones who knew the Donovan name and had already counted the dollar signs before smiling into the face of one of the illusive men; or naive and impressionable, those were the ones who didn't have a clue but would have a man so tied up in scandal and delusions of love affairs he wouldn't know what to do with himself.

No, Deena Lakefield was surprisingly different and refreshingly arousing.

Jogging down the front steps, he caught up with her just as the stone pathway turned to grass.

"Taking an afternoon stroll in lieu of the moonlight one you denied me last night?"

She turned, looked up at him, laughter already sparkling in her eyes. At her ears, large gold hoops dangled. "I didn't deny you anything. I just didn't feel like walking."

Max nodded, slowing his pace so that his long stride matched her short, quick one without missing a beat.

"I didn't ask you last night if you were here for just business or a little pleasure, too," he said, noting the quietness that surrounded them. There wasn't another house for miles and they were walking along the generous acreage of Sandy Pines. He wondered where she was going since he was currently following her lead. He knew which parts of the island he wanted to visit, needed to get around to visiting to secure the appropriate permits required to get started on the renovations. But for right now he was content to take some time to get to know her better. The slow Southern pace was doing something to him, something he wasn't sure he liked.

"A little of both. I can write anywhere, but my next book is set on a secluded island."

"Really? Does the hero save the heroine from a vicious shark attack? For which she must repay him by spending one glorious night in his bed?"

She stopped and used a hand to shade the sun from her eyes as she looked up at him. "Just how many romance novels have you read, Mr. Donovan?"

"I like it better when you call me Max." Reaching out, he took one of her hands in his and continued their walk. "And I don't read romance novels. The formula is just so cliché anybody would know it."

"That's not true. Granted, there are certain plots that work well over and over again. The author's goal is to not be cliché, to let the characters fall in love on their own."

"Yeah, with candlelight dinners and violinists in the background."

"Or something as simple as lovers walking on the beach."

Her words seemed to float on the breeze as the grass shifted to sand. Max looked to his left and saw that their walk had led them right to the shoreline. Broad Creek greeted him with glistening blue-green water and rustic sand. The sky was a periwinkle blue with the sun like a huge orange beacon in its center. The breeze was gentle, the air fresh. It was, Max thought, the perfect scene.

"Touché," he conceded her observation and continued walking along the sand. "So that was the business portion. What's the pleasure? Are you here alone?"

"Funny you should ask that now as you walk me along the beach, holding my hand like we've known each other a lifetime."

Max chuckled and felt more relaxed here with her at this very moment than he had in the last couple of years.

"I figure you're alone because what man would be foolish enough to let you out of his sight?"

"If you hadn't just told me differently I'd swear you've been reading romance novels. You've got sugary lines memorized."

"Not sugary. Honest."

"You make a habit of being honest?" she asked.

"I try. How about you?"

She shrugged. "It's the only way I know how to be. My family says I don't think before I talk, so you're never quite sure what'll come out of my mouth."

"I guess that can be a good and bad thing."

"I've never had any problems. It's mostly the person I'm talking to that doesn't like something I've said. But that's probably because the truth hurts."

"Yeah, sometimes I guess it does," he answered quietly.

"So you never said what you're doing here at the luxurious Sandy Pines."

"Originally this trip was all about work. But now," he said as they came to a stop, "it's definitely pleasure."

"Is your company thinking of buying a resort here?"

"My mother owns the Sandy Pines," he said, trying not to wince at the thought. However, after his complete tour of the grounds and a couple nights to really think about it, he was coming up with a strategy to make this an old Southern bed-and-breakfast exactly the way his mother remembered it.

"Really? So you're of high class after all," she said teasingly, remembering their conversation from last night. "Wait a minute, you said your name was Donovan, right? The oil tycoon Donovans?"

She'd turned so that instead of being beside him she was now standing in front of him.

He laughed. "One and the same."

"And that's funny?"

"No. I'm just glad you didn't say The Triple Threat Donovans."

"Really? Why?"

"They're my cousins, Adam, Trent and Linc. They sort of have a reputation for being unobtainable."

"All of the Donovan men have that reputation, as well as their relatives. I've heard all of this, not actually experienced it for myself. My sister is dating Sam Desdune. I think he's friends with one of your cousins. Anyway, he told us all about your family."

Max would have to remember the next time he saw Sam to jack him up for that little favor. "Sam's a good friend of the family. The private investigation business he and Trent run is doing really well. I heard he'd finally settled down." Another one in the growing list of relatives and close friends that were taking the leap, Max thought but didn't say.

"I like Sam and his family. Haven't met any of the other Donovans."

Unable to resist touching her, Max ran a finger up and down her bare arm. "So you'll base your judgment of them on me?"

She smiled. "No. Of course not. I'm sure they have no more control over you then my family wishes they had over me."

"For the most part my family's not like that. We pretty much do our own thing."

"Even if it's not in the family business?" There was something there in the shift in tone when she'd said that. It made Max think her life wasn't as happy as she seemed to be.

"Sure. My cousin Linc owns two casinos and is thinking about expanding overseas. Trent went into the Navy right out of high school and is now running a P.I. firm. Adam and I are in real estate. We've got a cousin in construction, one in finance. We're all over the place."

"And your family's cool with it. That's great."

"You sound like your family's not like that. Are you going against the grain by writing books instead of doing what they want?"

"Very perceptive, Donovan," she quipped.

"Max."

She nodded. "Right. Max. Yeah, my family's really different from yours. Well, at least my immediate family is. There's my parents, old-school money and by-the-book, who take working and succeeding very seriously. Then there are my sisters, both older, both more successful in my parents' eyes. But that's mainly because Monica and Karena went into the family business."

"Which is?"

"Oh, art. I thought I told you that already. We own the Lakefield Galleries of Manhattan and soon to be Atlanta with my cousin Simone at the helm. Monica runs the gallery like a private school nun and Karena does all the buying. They're both really good at what they do. The gallery is a huge success."

"And you write books. No interest in art at all, huh?"

She'd begun kicking at the sand. Her painted toes were now sprinkled with the grains. He suspected she didn't like the way her family treated her but that she got through it by putting up some sort of bravado.

"It's not that I don't like it. I mean, there are some really great pieces that I can appreciate. It's just not my passion. You know what I mean?"

What Max knew without a doubt was that this small, friendly woman was full of passion, whether it be in art or writing, it was there, and should definitely be appreciated.

"I know what it means to do something you really enjoy. Most people aren't that fortunate to have their dream job, so I'm grateful for my opportunity. You should definitely take advantage of yours and if your family doesn't understand, then that's their problem. Not yours."

"My sentiments exactly," she said with that infectious laugh of hers.

But Max sensed more. She didn't dismiss her family's treatment as easily as she appeared to. Then again, he'd only known her for some hours now, he could be totally wrong about her.

"I love birds," she said almost absently, looking up toward the sky.

Max followed her gaze. "And butterflies and moonlit walks."

"Yeah, and those too. But I really envy birds."

"Should I be afraid to ask why?"

"I don't get the impression you're afraid to ask or do anything, Max Donovan," she said honestly. There was just this air about him, this aura that seemed to surround him. Confidence. Power. Strength. All of which were filling her mind with serious hero possibilities. "I envy their freedom. They can fly anywhere they want, anytime they want. There's nobody to stop or prevent them from traveling, from doing their own thing. It's got to be a terrific feeling."

"I see your point," he said.

She wasn't really listening for his response, her attention really was on the birds she'd seen just a moment ago that now were just about out of sight. But there was no mistaking his hand releasing hers or his body shifting so that part of the bright sunshine and her precious birds were blocked from view. All she could see now was his face, his piercing eyes and tempting mouth. He was close enough so that the scent of his cologne mixed pleasantly with the water and sand aroma. His body was just broad enough, just muscled enough to make her feel sheltered, protected.

"I've been thinking of something else that might elicit a pretty good feeling."

Better than what she was feeling now that he had her sheltered by his arms? She could only imagine.

But even her imagination wasn't that good.

His head descended slowly, just enough to have her catching her breath. His lips touched hers in a whisper, like the barest summer breeze. Impatient and hungry for more, she came up on her tiptoes, wrapping her arms around his neck, opening her mouth to his. Their lips touched again, soft, slow. It was hard to follow his lead but his firm grip on her said that's the way he wanted it. She let him kiss her slowly again, just his lips. That small act stole her breath.

It seemed like a luxurious but painful forever before he deepened the kiss, his tongue moving slowly, erotically, over hers. It wasn't like a practiced dance or even a pleasant symphony, but more like a tidal wave of intense pleasure and longing. His palms flattened on her back, one moving just inches above her bottom. She pressed into him, or was he pulling her closer? She couldn't really tell, didn't actually care. All that mattered at this moment was the absolute perfect way in which Max mastered her mouth. It would have been like he was teaching her what he liked, except she felt like she already knew. The kiss was strangely familiar and yet the man was one she'd just met. It was beyond odd, but damned delicious so she wasn't about to complain.

When he finally pulled away from her Max wasn't sure what time of day it was or where they were for that matter. All he knew was that he definitely liked kissing Miss Deena Lakefield.

"That was better than looking at the birds," she said, her signature smile spreading quickly across her face.

Liking that smile and appreciating those lips even more he found himself chuckling. "I wholeheartedly agree."

Chapter 3

It was late afternoon by the time Max had finished walking the grounds of Sandy Pines and talking to some of the natives of the island. There were two other properties within walking distance of Sandy Pines. Well, they weren't actually in normal walking distance, a total of seven miles each way, but he was used to moving around and working out, so it hadn't bothered him.

He needed to get an idea of the tone of this island. What the people liked or didn't like. He wasn't shocked to learn there were lots of rules about building on the island, lots of restrictions he'd have to make sure he followed. While Hilton Head had been turned into a resort haven, the town still wished to hold on to its original small-town feel. As he walked back, looking at the magnificent scenery ideas for the new and improved Sandy Pines flowed through his mind.

Along with thoughts of a certain pretty woman. After their impromptu walk on the beach this morning she'd said she had to work. He understood as he was here to work as well, so they'd parted ways. But he'd thought of her on and off all day. It felt weird for Max to think about a woman this much, that wasn't his normal reaction to women.

As a Donovan he automatically had a reputation for being a playboy, even if it was unfounded. Unlike his cousins, he wasn't mentioned in the local gossip pages for his reputed womanizing. Here and there because he was a Donovan, his name would appear if he were at some big function or had a date that had a little popularity of her own. But that wasn't often and it wasn't a reputation Max tried to play to. On the contrary, he led a much more solitary and out-of-the-spotlight life than his more famous relatives. That was a purposeful move designed to protect not only himself but the women that he may become involved with.

Max's definition of being involved with a woman wasn't the same as the other Donovans either. He didn't do long-term, at all. Two to three dates max was about all he could manage. He wasn't a stranger to sex but didn't use that as a reason to scope out women either. No, Max was not the normal Donovan on the inside. On the outside was another story entirely. Then again, he knew that people were going to see what they wanted to see in a person. So the reputation preceded him, that didn't mean he had to live up to it.

It was a warm afternoon so since he'd worked for the better part of the day, Max decided to take a little time for himself. Leaving his room, he took a back staircase that led down to the first floor and a door that opened right up to the large pool at the back of the house. The water looked refreshing in the early summer heat of South Carolina. So, after dropping his towel on a lounge chair, he wasted no time diving in.

He was swimming underwater when a pair of legs caught his attention. Heading directly for them, he surfaced and was rewarded once again with one of the prettiest smiles he'd ever seen.

"Hi, again," she said with a little chuckle.

"Hello." Max grinned, a quick punch of lust landing in his gut. Was there anything this woman wore that didn't look absolutely sinful?

Her bikini top was a deep purple color this time, cupping high, full breasts that had his mouth watering. Through the crystal clear water he could see a skimpy bottom and swallowed to keep from drooling like a horny teenager.

"Great minds must think alike," he said.

"They must."

"I thought you were writing."

"It was too hot. I wanted to come outside, enjoy some of the scenery. Well, enjoy the pool." She laughed.

"I hear you, I couldn't resist it either."

"You have great form," she said.

He looked a little lost for a minute so she amended her words. "I watched you dive in. Do you swim often?"

He grinned. "Yeah. I try to hit the gym every day. A swim always follows my workout. What about you? How often are you at the gym?"

"How'd you know I go to the gym?" she wondered.

He took her wrist, lifted her arm out of the water into

the air. "This type of toning is not natural. So whatever you're doing in the gym, keep it up. You have a terrific body."

If she were hot from the temperature outside, Max Donovan had just wracked up the degrees with that comment. Deena had watched a little more than just his diving form when he'd joined her in the water.

She'd seen him the moment he stepped from the house. His trunks weren't anything fancy, but gave her a terrific view of his muscled thighs. A bare chest had every nerve in her body tingling and great biceps sort of topped the entire package off. He looked good but didn't carry himself like he *knew* he looked good. She liked that. A lot.

"Thanks," she responded. "You're not too bad yourself." She was trying to sound nonchalant, like she swam with gorgeous guys with enticing bedroom eyes all the time. Not!

They frolicked in the water awhile, racing each other, then dunking each other like little kids. Deena's side hurt from laughing so much. She was loving the idea of taking this trip now, despite what anybody else said, she had a feeling this was going to be a great summer.

And as she came up from another one of Max's sneak-attack dunks, his hands circled her waist, holding her close to the rigid contours of his body.

"I've never met a woman like you," he said, his pensive green eyes staring down at her.

She was nervous, but refused to show it. "Is that a good or bad thing?" she asked, treading water.

He licked his lips. "I'm beginning to think it's a really good thing."

His head began to lower and Deena's toes began to

tingle. Oh goodness, he was going to kiss her again. The kiss this morning still lingered on lips, another one would surely be the end of her.

"Good," she whispered seconds before his lips could touch hers.

"Very good," he said before sweeping his tongue over her bottom lip.

Her arms were reaching up to circle his neck immediately. He pulled her body even closer as he licked along her lips again. She trembled and opened her lips to him. But that wasn't what he wanted. Thrusting his tongue inside her mouth, he captured her tongue and suckled.

She would have sank right to the bottom of this pool with that quick erotic act if he hadn't been holding her so tightly against him. As it stood, all she could do was give herself over to his clever ministrations.

He took the kiss deeper, plunging her into a heated swirl of desire she'd never felt before. One of his palms went to her bottom as the other one centered in the middle of her back. She wrapped her legs around his waist and tilted her head to take some control over the drugging kiss.

In her mind it didn't really matter who controlled the kiss, all she knew was that she didn't want it to end. Maxwell Donovan was definitely a man she wanted to get to know better. In and outside of this pool.

"Time fo'te middleday meal. You just sit down. I'll be back in just a minute."

The next afternoon, Max led Deena to the large dining room table and, pulling out a chair for her, he obeyed the tall, military-looking woman's request. From her greeting the first day he'd arrived, he knew she was Dalila Contee, the supervising maid and cook. She'd been here at Sandy Pines for more than thirty years.

"What did she just say?" Deena asked when they were seated and alone.

"She said it's time for lunch. She's speaking part Gullah and part English."

"Gullah?"

Max nodded. "It's a popular language in the sea islands of the south. Slaves from the Sea Islands of South Carolina and northern Georgia were brought to America largely from different communities on the Rice Coast of West Africa. They spoke many different languages, so in order to communicate with each other they combined the similarities of their language with the English they learned and formed the unique Gullah language."

"Wow, I never knew that."

"Most people don't. I didn't until I started researching the island of Hilton Head. It has a rich history in our rise from slavery, one I'm thinking we should preserve."

"You're probably right."

"What other ideas do you have for Sandy Pines?"

There were already plates set on the table, good china, he surmised by looking at it closely. The glasses were most likely crystal, both in an older-looking pattern, that meant they'd been in this house and in his family for a while. It was certainly something to see firsthand some of what his ancestors had accomplished. Most people of African American descent didn't even know from where they came, let alone the opportunity to sit at a table that a great-grandfather had probably used.

"Right now I'm just getting a feel for the place, for the island. I think there's more here than history has told."

"I think you might be right," she agreed just before Dalila came back in.

"You Alma's boy. Same lukkha her," Dalila said, putting bowls on the table and smiling over at Max.

"You know my mother?" he asked.

Dalila nodded her head, her silver-streaked hair not moving at all as it was pulled back so tight into a bun. She wore a long dark skirt and crisp white blouse. No apron, no uniform, just clothes, understated but neat. There was an air of authority about Dalila, a no-nonsense aura that radiated from her. And there was knowledge. Max could see in her eyes that this woman had seen a lot, experienced a lot. And, yet, she was still standing. He both admired and envied her that.

"Alma was a good girl. Came here in the summer with her parents. Then wit' her chillun. Two boys. Max and Ben. Strong names she give you."

Max barely remembered their summer visits here. Now, he was embarrassed by that fact.

"Right," he said as a way of agreeing but not admitting. "Are you the only one left working here?"

He'd seen a groundsman around when he'd checked in and of course there was the young lady that had taken all his information and his credit card the minute he'd walked through the doors. But in the three days since he'd been here he hadn't seen anyone else.

"Old Juno takes care the outside. Me and Chiniya, Juno's girl, we take care of the inside. Don't need nobody else, don't get more'n two or three here a month.

You from the city too?" she asked, moving closer to Deena.

"Ah, yes. I'm from New York."

"Hm-hmm," Dalila said, crossing long arms over her ample breasts. "Need to take time out. Go to town, take 'em wid you. Attuh you eat."

As fast as she'd come in, Dalila left. Deena hummed happily, lifting a bowl and scooping potato salad onto her plate.

"What are you so happy about? She didn't have much to say to you."

Passing him the bowl she said, "I think she did. I mean, I don't think it's actually the words but what lies in between that she said. She thinks we work too much, don't take time to enjoy the scenery enough, wants us to go exploring after we eat. I'm with that."

Shaking his head, Max put potato salad on his plate, picked up a piece of fried chicken and put that on his plate too. For somebody who didn't know what the Gullah language was a few minutes ago, Deena sure had understood Dalila well. And she'd called him perceptive? No, Max was sure that Deena Lakefield saw more and deciphered more than anyone gave her credit for. Just another fascinating attribute that made her…what was she to him? Special? Unique?

He didn't quite know, but planned to find out.

"Tell me more about your family?" he asked while they ate.

"Not much to tell. Monica's my oldest sister but she thinks she's my mother. She's controlling and rigid in what she thinks is right. But I love her anyway."

"It's like that with family. We don't have to always

like them, but we love them. What about your other sister? She can't be that bad."

Deena shook her head. "Oh, no. Karena's great. She had a hard time last year when she hooked up with Sam because she didn't think she could be in a relationship and have a successful career. But she's gotten over that."

"Sam's a good guy. He'll treat her right," Max said, not really wanting to talk about relationships, but acknowledging that it was probably going to be a little hard to skirt around that issue.

"What's your family like? There are a lot of Donovans, I hear."

"There are. My uncle actually lives in Dallas but all three of his kids have left home. His wife died years ago so we always think he's alone, but he says he's just fine."

"Alone doesn't always mean lonely," she pointed out. "Some people just like to be by themselves. I think they can still lead normal lives that way."

"I agree," Max said because sometimes he felt more like his Uncle Albert than he was ready to admit.

"Do you like to be alone?"

He shrugged. "Sometimes. I mean, don't get me wrong, I love hanging with my cousins. We have a great time together. And I like our family gatherings. But there are times I just need to be alone. You know, with my thoughts and stuff."

"You look like a thinker," she said before taking a sip of her lemonade. "Like there's a lot on your mind that you're trying to sort out."

"It just seems easier to work things out that way."

"I'm the exact opposite," she told him. "I like to talk." Then she chuckled. "I guess you can tell that already."

He smiled. "It's okay. I just figured you had a lot to say."

"All the time," she added. "My mother said I've been talking since birth. I don't believe that but I was the first of her children to talk and walk. Like I've always had someplace I wanted to be or something to do."

"And you're on your way there with your writing?"

She sighed. "I love writing. It's like having the chance to escape into my own little world. I really enjoy the freedom and the expression. I believe this was my calling. Despite all the other things I've tried."

"Other things like what?" He wasn't sure but thought it might be a little dangerous asking this question.

"Hmm, let's see. I did a few months as a video dancer. Then I thought I might like acting. Those didn't really turn out to be my thing. I like to be in the spotlight somewhat. But the thought of people staring at me and my body shaking all the time wasn't very appealing. I tried catering, because I love to cook. But that required a little more organization than I could manage."

"You sound like quite the entrepreneur."

"I guess. But this is it, writing is the one. I have a really content feeling with this, a satisfaction all those other careers didn't give me. Monica calls me scatterbrained because I've moved from one thing to another for so long."

He put his fork down, seeing again that as much as she acted like it didn't bother her, what her family thought of her and said to her really affected her. "I don't think that makes you scatterbrained. If more people took the time to figure out what they wanted to do with their lives, the dropout rate in college wouldn't be so high. Companies wouldn't have an increased turnaround in staffing. Careers are big decisions and not everyone is born knowing what it is they want to do."

"Were you?"

He shook his head. "Actually, I studied engineering in college, thinking I'd build bridges or something like that. Who knew I'd get into sales and renovations. But, like you with writing, there's a satisfaction in what I do that I don't think I'd get from doing anything else."

"And your parents were fine with that?" she asked, still with doubt.

"I think parents just want what's best for their kids throughout their entire life. The problem is, what's best is not always what the parent sees. But it's okay, Deena, you don't have to walk anybody's path but your own. I'm sure your family will come around when they see how happy you are with your writing career."

"I hope so," she said but Max could tell she wasn't convinced.

That was unfortunate. One thing he knew for sure was that he didn't like this melancholy and doubting Deena. He liked her smiling and talking. So he'd just have to keep her mind on things beside her family and their thoughts about her career.

Right after lunch, after Dalila's second directive to do so, Max and Deena headed to Shelter Cove. Max drove the car he'd rented upon his arrival while Deena plotted their course using the map she'd gotten from her travel agent. What they both noticed first about their drive was that it was a little difficult spotting signage to help guide their way. According to town regulations, signage was limited in order to promote the island's natural beauty.

"We're lost," Deena said after they'd passed the same spot on US 278 three times.

"I am not lost. I have a GPS right here," Max said, tapping the dashboard. "And you have a map right there."

"And we're lost," she reiterated. Why men could never admit this was beyond her.

"Shelter Cove is just around this bend."

"You mean the bend we've been around three times already?"

He shot her an annoying glance and she smiled sweetly. "Why don't we stop at that gas station and ask directions?"

"Because I'm not lost," he said, stubbornly driving past said gas station.

A half hour passed and Deena had let her map slip to the floor. She knew they were lost, it was just about waiting until Max would admit it. So instead she turned on the radio, flipping past several stations. An oldie but goodie was on a station she passed and she hurriedly flipped it back. Luther Vandross's "A House Is Not a Home" played and Deena sang along.

For a while Max listened to her slightly off-key voice. This song had been an all-time favorite for him but he didn't say that. In fact, he didn't say a word, just let her sing until the song was finished.

"I take it you like that song."

"What? Are you kidding? Who doesn't like Luther and his many love ballads? Many of his songs have inspired some pretty hot love scenes in my stories."

"Really? You need Luther to inspire you to write love scenes? What about personal experience?"

"I have that, too. But nothing compares to Luther."

Was she always so open? Each time he asked her a question, she answered him. Never once did she hesitate. Max was used to women being calculating, manipulative, their every response practiced and designed to lead to what they ultimately wanted. He didn't get that impression from Deena. She just said whatever was on her mind. He wondered if that was a good or bad thing.

"Okay, you win," he said finally.

"I win what?"

"We're lost."

Deena laughed. "No, you're lost. I've just been waiting for you to realize it."

He couldn't be angry; her laughter was contagious. The mood was light. Being with her, pleasant. He decided to go with it.

Living in New York and Las Vegas, both of them were fairly used to shopping at high-end stores. When they'd finally reached Shelter Cove they were both in awe of the specialty shops like De Gullah Creations and Blue Parrot. Deena happily picked up souvenirs for both her sisters and her mother.

"Not getting your father anything?" he asked as they stepped up to the counter to pay.

"He wouldn't be interested in anything here," she answered quickly. "My father is very stern and very shrewd. He frowns upon what he calls frivolous spending."

Max nodded, pulling his wallet out of his pocket on instinct as the clerk gave Deena a total. "So he's tight?"

"No, I wouldn't say that. I guess he just wants to hold on to what he has."

"A closed fist never receives anything," Max said, extending his arm to give the clerk his credit card. "My mother used to tell me that when I was young."

"Oh. No, you don't have to do that," she said, pushing Max's hand away from the clerk. "I have money." She was digging through her purse for her wallet.

"It's okay. I want to pay for it."

"But you don't have to. I can pay for my own things."

The clerk looked from one of them to the other, huffing impatiently.

"Deena," Max said, putting a hand on her arm. "It's okay. I'll pay for the items." He sensed she was about to say something else so he continued, "You can buy me a soda and snack when we leave. I'm still hungry."

Reluctantly she put her wallet away, frowning up at him. "I'll buy you a snack and whatever else I decide to purchase, Mr. Donovan."

He opened his mouth to speak but she was the one to stop him this time. "I know. Max."

With another of her sugary smiles she took her bag and walked out of the store.

"Independent woman, huh?" the clerk asked.

"I guess so," was Max's reply. "Independent and sexy as hell."

Chapter 4

Meeting a guy in the middle of the night then letting him kiss her senseless on the beach the next morning wasn't out of the ordinary for Deena. The impulsiveness of the situation actually lived up to her reputation. Still, she had a good feeling about Max Donovan and she always trusted her gut. That's something her father taught her that she actually took to heart.

Now she was getting dressed to go to dinner with him. They'd shopped and toured the island all afternoon. Max needed to get a feel for the scenery to help him with the project he was doing for his mother. She just wanted to see the island, maybe get some ideas for her book. But mostly, she just didn't want her time with him to end, so she'd tagged along. Tonight was special, different. It was their first date.

They were going to Antonio's, an Italian restaurant at

the Village at Wexford. Dalila had recommended it and called to make reservations for them. Deena liked Dalila with her native language and no-nonsense demeanor. She was stern yet there was a feel of compassion from the woman, a line of gentleness Deena guessed most people missed in her. And because she liked studying people, prided herself on being an awesome judge of character, Deena took to the woman immediately. Whatever she said, Deena agreed with, to Max's dismay.

She figured Max liked Dalila, too, although he was spending way too much time trying to figure the woman out instead of just listening to what she was saying. After their jaunt through town, Dalila had given them more Gullah history, telling them how the Gullah people mostly lived by proverbs. They had a saying for almost everything, a meaning more diverse than some thought. It was intriguing to hear about this group of people, to know their rich history. Max did agree with her in that area, still he seemed to hold something back.

In contradiction, Max was very talkative about the rehab of Sandy Pines. His visions for the resort were commendable. Even Dalila sort of expressed her approval, with a grunt and some mumbled words. Even though he didn't like Dalila taking the decision from him, Max wanted to go to Antonio's. He'd said he wanted to get an idea of the locals as well as the tourists, what they liked, what they didn't like. All this was to make sure he was incorporating the right ideas into the new and improved Sandy Pines. For a while he sort of reminded her of Monica with the way he was focused on his job, but then she'd realized his focus was mainly due to the fact that he had a personal connection to this place. His mother. If there was one thing she knew for sure, which impressed her more than money or prestige ever could, it was that Max Donovan loved his mother fiercely. She could hear it in his voice when he spoke about her wishes for this house, could see it in his eyes when he looked at the house, the island. This project was important to him because it was his mother's property, it was a part of him.

So she took extraspecial care with her clothes and her hair and makeup. She wanted to look her absolute best. What did she expect to happen tonight? Another one of those toe-curling kisses would be good. Was it impulsive and maybe a bit irresponsible to think they might just end up in bed? Probably, but life was too short for hesitations. Deena had always thought that way. When she made up her mind to do something, she did it. Whatever was meant to be, would be. That was the whole concept behind fate, which she believed in inexplicably.

When she was pleased with her dress, her hair and the scent of the perfume she'd decided on, Deena grabbed her purse and was heading out of her room when her cell phone chirped, signaling she'd received a text message.

You didn't tell me you were leaving town. Call me. M

Oh, hell no. Talking to her was not fate, she refused to believe that. The very last person she intended to call at this moment was Monica. Her sister would surely try to put a damper on the good time Deena was having. Monica would tell her she was being foolish and reckless, going out with a man she hardly knew. But Deena did feel like she knew Max, indirectly, sort of. Max knew Sam, who was great and loved Karena to pieces. Max was a Donovan; they'd been respected for years in Texas, New Mexico and Nevada in the oil business as well as worldwide for their philanthropic efforts. They were an old, distinguished family with little to no scandal, that was what Monica was ultimately concerned with. Deena refused to succumb to the same paranoia or distrust about people that her sister had.

No, she definitely was not allowing Monica to interfere. Putting the phone on vibrate she tossed it back into her purse and headed downstairs to meet her date for the night.

"So how's it going?" Adam asked.

Rubbing a hand over his face in an attempt to refocus, Max answered, "As good as can be expected. I have a contractor coming out tomorrow afternoon just trying to jot down all the thoughts I have on the project."

Trying to keep his mind on the project and not on the gorgeous and seductively tempting Deena Lakefield was more like it. That was easier said than done. She was everywhere—on his mind, in the dining room, on the beach, in the car singing, at the store shopping—he couldn't escape her and wasn't sure he wanted to.

"Time projection?" was Adam's follow-up.

"Six months minimum. Hurricane season has just begun but I'd like to get done as much as we can before the storms start hitting the island. I don't know what's forecasted but I don't want to take any chances either."

"You're right, better to be cautious. What do you think the possibility of your mom keeping this place up and it running successfully is?"

"Hey, you know my mom, once she sets her mind to something, she makes it happen. I think with the right management down here it could be profitable. There's no real need for another resort, but I don't see that tourists will complain about having another option. The locals are fine with it as long as the look of the place stays true to the island heritage. And that's fine since it's precisely what my mother wants."

"Yeah, her and my mother have been talking a lot about the place. They're real excited. You know how that can be."

They both chuckled at the thought.

"How's Camille holding up?" Max asked. It was almost midnight in Rome. He wondered why Adam was on the phone with him instead of in bed with his pregnant wife.

"Going stir-crazy with excitement. She wants the international success and she wants the baby to be born healthy. I'm trying to get her to slow down, but you know how she is."

"Yeah, I do." Camille Davis-Donovan was a go-getter; she was ambitious and tenacious. And she was an absolute sweetheart. Max had liked her from the first time they'd met in the Donovan Investments conference room. She was perfect for Adam and he wished them all the best. "Maybe after the show you can talk her into taking some time off until after the baby's born."

"Already on it, man. I've talked to her doctor, who's going to suggest she go on bed rest until delivery. That'll give her at least eight weeks rest before the baby gets here. After that she's required to take another six weeks. I won't be able to hold her down much longer than that."

"Good luck trying to keep her down that long."

"I just want her to be healthy and I want the baby to be born safely, that's all."

Max nodded even though he knew Adam couldn't see him. "I know what you mean. She's your wife. You love her and want to protect her. I get it."

"Nah, I don't think you'll really get it until you're totally in love with a woman yourself."

And that was a subject Max definitely did not want to talk about. "On that note, I'll let you get to bed."

Through the other line Adam's chuckle made Max feel like they were both at home in Nevada sharing a normal conversation.

"Your time will come, cousin. Just you wait. There's a woman out there waiting especially for you."

As much as Max wanted that to be true, he was a realist. He knew his limitations and didn't wish them on anyone, especially not any woman. "I don't think so, but thanks for being so optimistic about my love life."

"Your love life's fine," Adam said. "It's your future happiness I'm worried about."

"I'm straight, man. No need to worry."

"Say what you want, but I know you."

He did. They were all as close as brothers—Henry, Albert and Everette Donovan's children had been raised like siblings. They were all close and all fiercely loyal to each other. Adam did know him, but he didn't know what was best for him.

"Go take care of your wife. I'll talk to you when you get back."

"I'll be back home before you most likely. But we'll touch base in a couple of weeks unless there's something urgent."

"Sure. Take care. Kiss Camille for me."

"Not a chance." Adam laughed. "You be safe and get out of there before any hurricanes hit."

Hanging up with Adam was like being a kid and leaving for camp for the summer. Waves of homesickness wracked him. He wanted to be back in his apartment, listening to the jazz CDs he loved, staring out at his view of mountains and desert. He wanted a glass of wine and the solitary confinement he'd resigned himself to.

And he wanted to go downstairs, meet Deena Lakefield and have a great evening with her.

Two sides to one coin, conflicting emotions, contradictory outlooks. What he would choose and what was the best choice were probably totally different.

Yet he stood, checked himself out in the mirror one more time, then left his room.

He had a dinner date. For better or for worse.

"Tell me the craziest thing you can think of about yourself," Max said, thoroughly enjoying his glass of red wine after their meal of shrimp primavera.

Deena hesitated for the briefest of moments before a huge grin spread across her face. "When I was in high school I was a cheerleader."

"Not that crazy. I can actually see that." And he could visualize her in a short skirt and tight sweater, dancing around the football field with a smile on her face and that tight little body enticing every guy in sight.

"That's not all. The captain of the cheer team was Brittany Baines, who thought she was 'it' with a capital *I*. Brittany had been dating the captain of the basketball team before he wised up and decided to get his goodies elsewhere. Well, he was still getting his goodies from a member of the cheer team, just not from Brittany. Anyway, Brittany was all pissed about the break up and making the rest of the team's life a living hell because of it. So we were all sick of the six-hour practices seven nights a week and Brittany's overall bitchy attitude. We were all seniors but Brittany was the only one psyched about going to college to cheer competitively. Rumor was that a scout from some college in Florida, I think, was at the game that night. We all decided this was our time to get revenge on Brittany. So as we were doing our opening cheer, we were all supposed to either moon or flash the crowd, right where the scout was supposed to be sitting."

Max shifted uncomfortably in his chair as this story had taken a turn he wasn't quite prepared for. The visual coupled with the one he was already having about her in a skimpy cheerleading outfit had his arousal growing. He lifted his glass to his lips because his mouth had suddenly gone very dry.

"See, the idea was that as the captain, Brittany should have a certain amount of control over her squad. I know it was lame and we weren't really considering that this could end her competitive cheering dream totally. We just wanted a little taste of revenge against her." She took a sip of her wine, swallowed and continued, "Apparently, I was in the company of a bunch of chickens because when the time came I was the only one who lifted her shirt, baring my twenty-eight B's to the entire crowd."

The sip he'd just taken of his wine went down the wrong way and he began to cough. She was up and around the table in no time, lifting one of his arms in the air and simultaneously smacking her other palm against the center of his back. People at other tables turned to stare at him and a waiter came hustling over.

"Are you all right, sir? Should I call for assistance?"

"No, he'll be fine. Just went down the wrong pipe," she said as his coughing slowed.

She was no longer clapping him on the back, but her hand was still there, moving in smooth circles. Feeling like an idiot, Max put his arm down and cleared his throat. "I'm fine. Just fine," he reiterated for the waiter, who looked as if he were about a second away from calling 911.

Going back to her seat, Deena picked up her own glass for a drink. When she was finished and with a mischievous gleam in her eyes, she asked, "Was that crazy enough for you?"

"What high school did you go to and what year did you graduate? And why wasn't I there?" he asked her, managing a smile of his own. Hell, yeah, that had been crazy enough for him. So crazy he was wishing he'd been a senior at her school at the time.

"I graduated in 1999. And it was a great year. Actually, I loved high school altogether."

"You graduated when? How old are you?"

"Twenty-nine. Why? How old did you think I was?"

"Ah, I hadn't really thought about it." This was true, not until this moment and this conversation had he thought about her age.

"Do I look older?"

"No. I didn't say that." He shrugged. "You look just fine."

"Just 'fine' like okay or 'fine' like you want to have me for dessert?"

If he'd been taking another drink he would have

surely choked again. Wisely, he'd left his glass alone. "You're candid, that's for sure."

It was her turn to shrug. With her fork she speared a shrimp, stuck it into her mouth and chewed. "Why beat around the bush?" she said after swallowing. "I'm attracted to you. Are you attracted to me?"

Using his napkin to wipe his mouth, Max sat back in his chair. Staring at her, he wondered if he'd ever met a woman like her before and quickly decided, no, he hadn't. "Yes," he answered simply. "I think I am."

"Good." She smiled. "And since you don't look old enough to be my father, I'm going to assume that since we're both consenting adults, we're free to act on that attraction. Am I right?"

"I'm thirty-five years old." Saying it aloud made him feel centuries older. Candidness worked well for her; for him, not so good.

"See, not old enough to be my father. Now, I guess the only other obstacle would be if you had a girlfriend or a wife. I don't see any rings, but then you could be one of those guys that doesn't wear a wedding band."

"If I were married I wouldn't be one of those guys. I would wear my ring. Proudly," he added.

"Are you thinking about marriage one day?"

"I'm not opposed to the institution," was his answer.

"Me either. My parents have been married a long time. I think long marriages are great, two people so totally dedicated to each other and their families. It's a wonderful thing."

"You thinking about having a family of your own?" He'd asked the question but wasn't entirely sure he wanted the answer. It shouldn't matter to him what her response was. It didn't. They were both here temporarily.

"I'd love to have a family. A husband and kids of my own along with a great career. I think I'd finally be content then."

"You're not content with your life now?"

"I wouldn't say that. I just know that there's something more out there for me. I just have to wait my turn to get it. Patience isn't one of my strong points."

"I'd think a writer would have to be patient."

"That's true. Nothing in the literary industry happens overnight. So yes, I've waited a long time to see my work published. And I've been waiting even longer to find an agent. But I'm learning to make good use of the time I spend waiting."

"Oh really? And how are you doing that? Or should I say, are you doing that with someone else?"

She licked her lips and everything inside him tightened. Blood pulsed but it wasn't throughout his veins. No, all of it had pooled in a nice heated spot, lengthening his arousal to painful proportions.

"If you're asking do I have a man back home, the answer is no. I'm blissfully single at the moment."

"Thank you, Lord." Max smiled. Deciding a drink was definitely in order, he lifted his glass of wine to his lips and took a slow sip.

She mimicked his motions with a thank you of her own. From that moment on he knew where they were headed and that it would be a night he'd never forget.

Chapter 5

Deena had done a lot of things in her young life, taken a lot of risks with herself and sometimes others. Sleeping with Max Donovan didn't seem that bad. He was a good-looking man that appealed to her on many different levels. He was smart and tenacious. He knew his job well, she supposed since he'd been working so hard to get Sandy Pines up to par with his mother's wishes. He was obviously dedicated to his family. That touched a special place with her because for all her family—Monica and her father, especially—gave her a hard time about her life's choices, they loved her. And she loved them. There was no question that they would each do anything for the other. Never had been. That's just the way the Lakefields were. The more time she spent with Max, the more stories she heard about him and his family, she got the sense they were the same way.

So why not sleep with him?

With no logical reason to stop her, she'd already changed into a clingy, short pink nightie. They were in her room and Max was waiting just outside the door. For some reason she wanted this night to be special, romantic. It was her summer fling, her "what happens in Hilton Head, stays in Hilton Head" moment and she fully intended to take advantage of the opportunity presented.

As for what would happen afterward, she had no idea. That didn't mean she hadn't already fantasized— because she had. Writing about two people falling in love kept her mind on romance and relationships. But not until now, not until meeting Maxwell Donovan did she have that tingle of something new, that extremely giddy feeling of fresh starts and endless possibilities. Max was definitely a possibility.

This was a mistake.

A huge mistake.

If he called home to any one of his cousins and asked their advice, each of them would say the same thing. She's too young. Too impressionable. This could end badly.

He knew that, kept replaying it over and over in his mind.

And yet he was still here.

Dinner had been nice, their open conversation about their mutual attraction a little uncomfortable at first, but then relieving. He didn't have to wonder if she was feeling him, even though he knew she was. Didn't have to worry about whether or not he was moving too fast for her. The age thing was an issue with him. Not to mention the fact that she was looking for happily ever after. He should have known that from the start. She was a writer, after all. Of course she'd be looking for the ending of her stories, how else could she write them over and over again? How else could she write them so well? After the first night they'd met he'd gone online, looked up her book and ordered it. After the next-day delivery, he'd finished the two-hundred-and-seventy-eight page novel in one night and admitted—only to himself—that he'd enjoyed it. She'd masterfully written a love story that would touch many hearts. It had touched his, in a remote sort of way. He could see the allure of such a story. And he could also see the dream of a young woman trying to find that same happiness.

A happiness he could never give her.

But this was just for tonight. They would sleep together, they'd agreed to that much. In the morning things would be just like yesterday. He'd be here to work on improving Sandy Pines and she'd be here to work on her novel.

It was simple, like riding a bike, Max thought, opening the door to the small balcony and stepping out. The evening air was sultry, the pool below enticing.

"Max."

The sound of her voice had him turning. And the simplicity of having sex with Deena Lakefield disappeared.

She'd poured her tight little body into a satin ensemble that was clearly created to make a man ache. His body tensed in response, arousal taking heated control over his senses.

"Come here," was all he could mutter.

She walked slowly, as if she knew the pace would cause him more turmoil. He ached, his fingers itching to touch, to explore. He leaned against the railing, attempting a casual, controlled demeanor. The moment she was close enough he inhaled her scent, let it drift along his heightened senses.

"You still want me for dessert?" she asked, her voice husky with desire.

He slipped his hands around her waist, lifted her until she wrapped her legs around him, then whispered against her lips, "Dessert. A nightcap. Breakfast." He kissed her, let his tongue linger with hers then pulled away. "Lunch. Dinner. Dessert again."

His mouth devoured hers, making the kiss a hungry exploration. She pressed her center against him, her breasts tingling as they pushed against his chest. His hands cupped her bottom, gripping it tightly. Her hands were frantic, cupping the back of his head, dancing along his shoulders. Their mouths seemed fused together, desperation coming in heavy pants of breath.

Her heart pounded in anticipation. His beat rapidly against her chest. Then his teeth were scraping along her jawline, down her neck. She arched her back, gave him full access as his mouth covered one nipple. Even through the satin she felt the scorching heat of his tongue, the marvelous waves of sensation that rippled through her body as his teeth snagged her nipple lightly. He opened his mouth again, released her nipple then sucked her breast greedily.

"Max." His name was a tortured whisper as her center pulsated with need.

He was going too fast; this was happening too fast.

Her voice echoed in his head, fierce arousal gripped his body, but his mind ached for more. With careful strides he carried her into the bedroom, laying her down onto the bed slowly.

His fingers went to the buttons of his shirt, but she came up on her knees, pushing his hands away. "Let me," she said, licking her lips in anticipation.

Max dropped his hands to his side, let her have her way. She undressed him, small nimble fingers, clearing the shirt from his chest, unbuttoning his pants and pushing them along with his boxers down past his waist. She slipped off the bed to handle his shoes and socks before he could step out of the clothes. When she was back on the bed his hands gripped her shoulders and he bent forward, ravishing her mouth one more time.

Before she could toss his pants he'd reached into his pocket and retrieved a condom. He was about to push her back on the bed when she snatched the condom away from him, slipping her hands between their bodies to cup his length. "I've wanted you since the first night I saw you standing in the kitchen."

If he were a lesser man Max would have yelled his release right then and there as she worked the latex onto his length. But he was a Donovan, he was a virile, strong man with a reputation of giving women exactly what they needed in the bedroom. No way was this little tigress going to undo him.

"And you always get what you want?" he asked.

"Aiming high usually brings good results," she whispered against his chest. Her tongue drew a long lazy path over his pectorals.

Not willing to tempt fate a second longer Max

removed her fingers from his erection and lay her back on the bed. "My turn."

The nightgown was shamelessly small, a wisp of material that he'd lifted over her head quickly. Her breasts were perfect mounds designed to fit his hand perfecty—as he lifted a palm, put it over the darkened nipple. She arched into his touch and he swore he'd never seen anything as beautifully seductive as this woman. Her springy curls framed her face, eyes half-closed, swollen lips parted so that her tongue could slide out to entice him further. The thong matched her nightie and Max traced a finger over the alluring lace. Her legs parted as she opened for him. His finger slid along the rim of the thong into her slickness of its own accord.

She was hot, tight and gripping him with intense suction. His erection grew to the point of pain and he gritted his teeth.

"Now," she panted.

"No," he responded quickly. His finger was driving her harder as he watched her control breaking into tiny pieces.

She writhed beneath him, her breath coming in quick pants. With his other hand he worked her breast, loving the soft full feel in his hands. He was in control, he was taking her the way he wanted. She wasn't getting the best of him. No matter how much he wanted to sink his length inside her.

When she screamed his name and her release poured into his palm Max was totally satisfied and about to explode with pleasure himself.

"Good girl," he cooed against her ear before nipping her.

"Let's make it better," she said, shifting so quick Max had to blink the moment he was flipped onto his back.

How she'd wrapped her legs around him and switched their positions so agilely he'd never know. But she was now on top of him, a victorious and sex-filled look in her eyes. She didn't waste time removing the thong, but pushed the material aside as she rose over him, gently lowering herself until he was snuggly inside.

She rode him like a practiced jockey. Only the thought of her doing this to some other man wasn't on Max's mind. The expertise with which she worked him, rising then falling at all the right times, had his mind filling with her. When he reached up, grabbed her hips to control the motions, she let her head fall back and called his name again. The way she said it made him feel like a superstar, like a hero in one of her books. It was all about him. And her. Together. At this moment.

It was surreal and then again it was just perfect.

She was very good, Max had to give her that. But he wanted to bring this home himself. So they shifted again, until he was sitting and she was straddling him. He pressed deep inside her, she wrapped her arms tightly around his neck. Their lips met as their bodies joined and moved in sync to the timeless dance of lovemaking.

They stayed like that for what seemed like forever. Deena's heart was beating rapidly, her body trembling with pleasure. It was him. He was it. Never, ever, had she had sex like this. It had to be more than sex, had to linger right around the lovemaking mark. That wasn't logical. It wasn't realistic. And yet it just was.

When he emptied himself into the condom she'd opened her mouth to scream his name but nothing came out. Instead she'd only been able to lower her head, dropping wet kisses along his shoulder.

It was perfect, just as she'd thought it would be.

Max sat at the homey kitchen table in the morning sun. It wasn't quite seven yet and Deena was anything but an early riser. But he enjoyed the morning. It was quieter then and he could get a lot of work done.

Not that he hadn't been able to work in the week and a half since he'd met Deena. She was about her business as well, so a couple afternoons they'd actually spent working. Her with her laptop and him with his. They would sit at the pool or on the wide wraparound porch with tall glasses of fresh-squeezed lemonade, courtesy of Dalila, served via Chiniya with her ready smile and bright intelligent eyes.

Their time seemed to be perfectly split between business and pleasure here at Hilton Head. Max wondered if it was just the Southern air that made him feel right at home. Someone else had other ideas.

"You know I been here since your granddaddy owned the place. He gave it to his sister when he passed, God rest his soul. Those were the good days."

Dalila was a regular fixture of Sandy Pines. So much so that even with the new plans, Max was positive his mother would keep the woman here to run the place. In actuality, he couldn't think of a better supervisor. Dalila would make sure things were done the right way. She loved this house and the land in a way Max doubted any college-degreed, managerially-trained, suit-and-tie-wearing person could.

"Did he stay here often? My grandfather?" Max asked.

Dalila had a way of skipping from one subject to another in the blink of an eye. It had taken Max a couple conversations to catch on to that and to learn to move with the flow.

"Spent every summer here with his chilren. Your mother was here with her sisters and brothers and they run all over dis island." Dalila laughed, her broad shoulders shaking with the effort. "Those was good times. Nobody come here no more. Not family, I mean."

"My mother's cousins, they didn't bring their family here?"

"Nope. And you boys stop coming too."

Max nodded. It had been years since he'd been here. But something told him it wouldn't take that long for him to return.

"Well, I'm trying to fix that. When we're done fixing up this place you'll have customers every week. This place is going to be wall-to-wall people."

"But is it gone be the right people?"

"What do you mean?"

"I means, everybody that can pay don't really need to be here. This here place is for families and young peoples in love or startin' families. Not all that work and stuff you and that little gal keep doing. It's for relaxin' and just being."

"I'm trying to make this one of the key vacation spots on the island. You disagree with that?"

"No," she said, shaking her head, her hair pulled back so tight not one piece of it moved with the motion. She came over to the table. She'd been at the sink snapping green beans for the dinner tonight, he supposed. Now she was right in front of him, leaning over the table, her wide hands flat on the surface.

"You can't make this place nuthin'. It just is. If you would open your eyes you could see that and a lot more."

Before he could think better of it, Max asked, "A lot more like what?"

"Like that gal that's got stars in her eyes cuz a you. You don't even know she in love wit you, do you?"

"Who? Deena? We're not in love, we're just…just—"

"Hmph, just what? Come see ein like come stay."

"Excuse me?"

"I says, come see in, like you foolin' around wit her ain't like come stay, as in you marry her right proper."

Max sighed, tired of this conversation already.

"We're not—"

"Mishmash," she said, interrupting him and throwing her hands up in the air. She was back at the sink snapping those beans with a heated urgency that made Max wonder if he'd eat them later. "Don't know what you feelin' or how to han'le it. More than what meets the eye, I tell you. More, much more. That gal ain't gone play with you while you figure it out either."

Max figured it was better to just not continue this particular conversation with Dalila. He and Deena were not in love. Yes, they were lovers, but that was just chemistry.

"Hey, baby," Deena said, entering the kitchen at the precise moment Dalila had slammed her bowl of beans down and walked out the back door.

She leaned over and kissed him on the cheek. "So what are we doing today? It's kind of hot out. I was thinking of maybe taking a swim. Or we could go into town again, do some more shopping?"

Max was only half listening.

This whole scene was a little too domestic, too practiced, too permanent.

Could Deena really be in love with him?

No. She was not that kind of woman. Well, actually… she hadn't mentioned any commitments but Max knew that eventually she did want to be married and have kids. She'd told him this on more than one occasion. He'd played it off, of course, because that was an impossibility. But now…now he wondered just what Deena thought they were doing.

And if their answers were different, what would happen next?

A few weeks later Max and Deena were still at Sandy Pines, researching and working most of the daylight hours—kissing and lovemaking throughout the night.

Today was the Fourth of July and a huge celebration was planned throughout the entire island.

"You two been spending lota time in da bedroom. Go out tonight, sit on da beach. Git some air," Dalila said in her normal, deadpan tone. But there was a twinkle in her eye tonight; Deena hadn't missed it.

She wasn't missing much these days. Her story was coming along beautifully, with Max unwittingly playing the new hero in her book. Joanna was falling hard for her new man, just as Deena was. She hadn't spoken to either of her sisters or her parents in the entire time she'd been here. Sure, she'd sent weekly emails to let them know she was still breathing, but she didn't want to talk to them. Surprisingly, her father had sent her one in response. He wasn't pleased with how long she'd been away—it was worrying her mother. And he didn't think using the excuse of working on another sex book was good enough for a grown woman to ignore her family.

Reading that message had ticked her off. Knowing that she didn't have to answer it and that right downstairs was a terrific man who actually applauded her entrepreneurial efforts made her smile. Deleting that email only confirmed she'd made the right decision in not calling home. She couldn't tell her family how much fun she was having for fear their negativity would jinx the entire affair.

Was this what they were having? An affair?

In the weeks since they'd first met she and Max had shared a lot about each other, their pasts, their present, their future goals and aspirations. But he hadn't said anything about what would happen when he returned to Las Vegas. And she hadn't considered when she would go back to New York.

She was a writer so she could work anywhere. If he asked her to go back to Las Vegas with him, would she go? Damn right she would. Being with Max felt too right to be wrong.

With her mind made up to simply enjoy the time they had together, Deena had dressed in a knee-length white sundress and accessorized with red-and-blue earrings, bangles and shoes. She'd happily climbed into the rental car with Max and hummed along cheerfully with the radio as they drove.

They were headed to the stretch of public beach where just one of many celebratory events was being held tonight. Dalila had packed them a basketful of food, that Max carried while she trotted behind him with blankets.

"You sure you're okay?" he asked when they'd found a spot.

She didn't sigh, even though she wanted to. This was the third time he'd asked her this since they'd left the house. "I'm fine, Max. Stop asking me that before I develop a complex."

"You just look like you're someplace else. And I want you to be here," he said, pulling her down on the blanket he'd laid out.

She chuckled. "I'm right here," she said, looping her arms around his neck and snuggling closer to him. "For as long as you want me."

She thought she felt him stiffen at that but then the fireworks began and people all around them cheered. Breaking away, she pulled some things out of the basket and they ate and watched the show.

"I love it here," she said after a while.

He nodded. "It's a nice vacation spot."

"Yeah, but it's more. Don't you feel it?"

Again, he hesitated.

"Sandy Pines will get a lot of tourists searching for this type of getaway."

"Sure they will," she responded. For all that Max had been asking if she were okay, Deena wondered if he wasn't the one preoccupied.

"When does your next book release?" he asked after a few minutes of silence.

"February."

"Just in time for Valentine's. Good marketing."

"February is the month for love."

"Is that what you're looking for? Love?" he asked quietly.

For the first time in her life Deena actually paused, considering what she would say. "Aren't we all?"

He shrugged.

"Look," she said, pointing upward toward a huge burst of fireworks. "It's pretty."

"Yes, you are," Max said.

Deena turned to find him not looking up at the sky but at her. She blushed and tried to look away but he reached up and touched her chin, keeping her facing him.

"I'm glad we met," he said seriously. "I'm really enjoying our time together."

"Me too," she said with a sigh.

Pulling her down until she was half on top of him, Max kissed her. The soft simple gesture quickly turned heated, urgent and she found herself ultimately splayed across him, returning his kiss with equal fervor.

"Not on the beach," he groaned when her hands had moved beneath his shirt to caress his chest.

They'd found a more secluded part of the beach and since there was more than one celebration going on throughout the island, their little beach wasn't that crowded.

"Scared?" she teased.

"No, but I'm not into sharing," he said, nipping her bottom lip. "Let's go."

They packed in record time and headed for the car. When Deena moved to the front passenger side door Max grabbed her by the arm.

"Back here," he whispered against her ear.

Max got in the backseat first, pulling her onto his lap before closing the door.

"In the car?" she asked as she straddled him in the backseat.

With both hands Max cupped her face, pulled her closer. "Scared?"

Slipping her hands between them, she undid the snap of his shorts, pulled the zipper down to release his heated arousal. "Not at all."

They were parked near the thick crop of trees just before the shoreline. It was beyond dark down this end of the lot and most people had walked to the beach anyway.

"I don't normally do this," he said, reaching up her dress to cup her bottom.

"Neither do I," she said, shifting quickly so that his length was instantly aligned with her arousal. He'd pushed the rim of her thong aside so that all he had to do was thrust forward. All she had to do was slide down.

They both moaned.

"There's a first for everything," he whispered, burying his face into her neck as he thrust inside her again.

"Definitely," she replied, letting her head loll back.

He held her hips, pulling her up and down on his rigid arousal. She groaned against the pleasurable sensation, desperately needing the release he seemed to be working toward.

"Deena," he whispered her name.

"Yes, baby," she answered.

"You're the best, this summer has…been the best."

He'd picked up his pace so his words seemed choppy, but she'd heard them just the same. Her heart soared even as pleasure rippled through her body. She wanted to respond but could only manage a few words. "Best. Yes, the best."

Through the material of her dress he opened his mouth over her nipple, suckling as he continued to pump feverishly inside her. Her heart hammered in her chest as she tried to keep up, tried to focus on the sensations, on what he was saying, what she was feeling. It was all too much, everything seeming to overflow inside her at once.

She screamed his name then clamped her mouth shut, hoping nobody heard her. Max groaned, gripped her bottom tightly and she knew his release had come as well.

It was a few more minutes before they both caught their breaths, then shuffled around the backseat trying to fix their clothes.

"Necking in the backseat of a car. Deena Lakefield, you should be ashamed of yourself," Max joked as they stepped out of the car and moved to the front door.

Slipping into the passenger seat, Deena laughed. "You're the oldest, I'm just following your lead."

Starting the car, Max laughed with her as they carried the romance of an evening on the beach and the intense arousal of a quickie in the backseat of a car back to the hotel.

Later that night Max lay in his bed, dosing off with Deena wrapped naked in his arms. His eyes were closed, his breathing growing slower as sleep began to approach.

Deena's face lay against his bare chest as she listened to the rhythmic sound of his heart beating.

All the while her heart filled, so much so words were

spilling out of her mouth without thought. "It could be like this forever with us. I love you, Max Donovan."

His heart almost stopped, his eyes struggling to open. His brain warned against both actions and he focused on keeping his breathing steady, his eyes closed. "I love you, Max Donovan." The words echoed in his mind and like a movie on fast-forward scenes flipped through his conscience.

Deena in love with him.

Deena trying on a wedding gown.

Deena walking down the aisle.

Deena tossing a pregnancy test into the trash can, tears in her eyes. For the umpteenth time.

His teeth gritted, every muscle in his body going rigidly still. He'd done something he swore he'd never do.

He'd messed up.

Big-time.

Chapter 6

December—Manhattan, New York

"I'll call you."

Those were the last words she'd heard from Maxwell Donovan, five months, three days and fourteen hours ago.

Every day Deena woke up she said she wasn't going to think about it, wasn't going to give him the pleasure of her thoughts. And every day she lied.

Today she was having brunch with her mother and sisters. This was their monthly get-together, a way of keeping in touch through everyone's busy schedule. Well, it was Noreen Lakefield's way of keeping tabs on her daughters. Driving out to Karena's home that she shared with Sam in Connecticut was peaceful except for the traitorous radio that seemed to play that Luther

Vandross song every time she turned it on. Now in silence she had no choice but to think about where she was in her life at this moment.

She'd finally finished her second book as hard as it had been. She couldn't write about her hero without thinking about Max. And thinking about Max had her heart breaking all over again. Her editor loved the story, said it was dripping with emotion and that the ending was so much more satisfying because of it. This may have been her best book yet. That should have made her happy. Instead she wanted to put the story out of her mind. She didn't anticipate working on the edits for the project or even promoting it for that matter. The memories were still too fresh, the wound too deep.

Monica said it was her fault. "That's what you get for being hot to trot," were her exact words. "I told you men weren't worth the breath it took to speak their names. But you never want to listen to me."

And she still didn't, Deena thought. She didn't want to hear I told you sos and so on. She just wanted the ache in her chest to go away.

Pulling up into the driveway she stepped out of the car and was instantly greeted by Romeo and Juliet, Sam and Karena's Great Danes. The friendly dogs loped beside her, both vying for her attention as she reached down and scratched behind their ears, cooing to them enthusiastically. Knocking on the door, she waited and was greeted by a smiling Karena.

"Hey, girl. What took you so long? Mama's been worried about you."

Karena gripped her in a hug as soon as she stepped into the foyer. "I was just running a little late. Tired, couldn't get out of bed."

Keeping her hands on her shoulders, Karena stood back enough so that she could stare into Deena's face. "Are you sick?"

"No."

"Pregnant?"

"God, no!" Zero sex in five months meant zero chance of a baby. Even though she couldn't say a part of her hadn't hoped.

The last night they'd been together in Hilton Head, the Fourth of July, they hadn't used any protection. For the first few weeks after she'd returned, Deena had entertained the idea of carrying Max's child. Unfortunately—or fortunately considering the way things had turned out between them—she wasn't pregnant.

Karena paused, then touched a hand to Deena's face. "Still heartbroken." It was a statement, not a question. As if her own sister didn't have any faith that she'd get over this man.

"I'm fine," she said, pulling away and going into the den.

The sooner she got this meal over with the better.

At a large oak table that sat on a platform near the patio doors, Noreen Lakefield sat with her oldest daughter. They looked a lot alike, Deena thought as she stared at them. Monica was the lightest in complexion, with her butter-toned skin, while Noreen's creamy brown tone highlighted her Native American heritage. They had the same dark, wavy hair, Noreen's streaked with a sterling gray. Monica's was pulled back into a tight bun, which was customary for her, and wrapped so tight nobody would guess it hung to the middle of her back. Of course, Monica had a sterner look to her as she leaned back in her chair, checking her watch.

"Sorry, I was running a little late." Deena knew what Monica would say before she'd even said it.

"You should strive to leave your house earlier instead of later," Monica said, lifting one brilliantly arched eyebrow. "What's wrong? You don't look good," she said as Deena pulled out a chair to take a seat.

"Gee, thanks," Deena said drably. "Hi, Mama."

"Deena," Noreen started, reaching across the table to take her hand. "Are you feeling okay?"

"Gracious," Deena sighed and pulled her hand from her mother's. She sat back in her chair, rolling her eyes toward the ceiling. "I am fine. Not sick. Not tired. Not heartbroken. Just fine." Her tone was brisk enough that everyone exchanged looks instead of speaking another word on the subject.

"Okay, so I have an announcement." Karena happily moved on to the next subject.

"So do I," Noreen added. "But you go first."

Thankful, Deena looked to both of them and smiled. "Good news, I can tell by the look on your face," she said to Karena.

"Excellent news! Sam proposed," she said, her smile bright enough to lift Deena's mood.

"Again?" Monica asked flatly.

"Yes, again. But this time I said yes! And look what he gave me!" Karena thrust her hand to the center of the table. Deena was the first to jump up and take hold.

"Awwww, that's beautiful," she said, admiring the princess-cut diamond solitaire and ignoring the pang of jealousy deep in her gut.

It was Monica's turn to take Karena's hand. "Just a

solitaire. I expected him to go all out since he's been asking you for almost nine months now."

"Oh, hush, Monica. It's beautiful," Deena said.

"I know. I love it," Karena gushed. "And I love him. I'm so happy."

And she should be, Deena thought. Her sister so deserved this happiness. She'd waited a long time for it and Sam was good for her. They'd be wonderful together. So Deena would just have to get over her irritable mood.

At the end of the table Noreen's eyes glistened. "It's beautiful, baby. You're a very lucky woman to have a man love you enough to be patient."

"So when's the big day?" Deena asked, trying valiantly to get excited about her sister's announcement.

"I'm thinking maybe next August. We have two big exhibits coming up that I don't want to interfere with," Karena said.

Monica nodded, reached across the table and poured herself a glass of orange juice. "That's right. The African Tribal Exhibit and Leandro's first formal showing. I need you focused on both of those."

"I know. I know. Besides, we want a huge outdoor event with all our family around us. Of course, you two will be maids of honor and I think Sam's sister Bree will be a bridesmaid."

"We can get Reverend Stubbing to do the ceremony," Noreen said. Then she reached into her purse and pulled out her date book. "I'll make a note to call him next week to check his availability."

"I'm not wearing yellow. That is not negotiable. And nobody does wedding dresses like Vera Wang, you should look into that quickly," Monica said, putting a bagel and fruit onto her plate.

"Actually, I have a few CK Davis dresses and was thinking about contacting Camille Donovan to see if she would design the gowns. Sam knows the Donovans really well. He thinks it's a great idea."

"So are we doing everything Sam says now?"

Monica seemed extra snippy today. Normally she was just part bitch. Deena and Karena exchanged a look, obviously both thinking the same thing—that Monica needed to get some, soon!

"Maybe Carolina blue?" Karena asked, totally ignoring Monica's other remarks. "What do you think, Deena?"

She'd been trying not to, if truth be told. As happy as she was for her sister, Deena really wasn't feeling up to talking about wedding plans when she couldn't even get the guy she was hung up on to call her back.

"Ah, blue is nice. Or green," she offered, trying to get into the swing of things. It wasn't like her to let emotions get the best of her. She was the smile-and-keep-it-going sister. Nothing ruffled her feathers, spoiled her day, rained on her parade. She was always in a good mood. That's what everyone expected of her. She couldn't let them down.

"Green is such a cheerful color," Deena said with a smile.

Monica frowned. "It's the color of grass and puke."

"Sage green would be nice," Noreen added.

The wedding talk went on for the next hour, until they were all stuffed and had debated just about every color in the rainbow.

Then Noreen cleared her throat. "I have an announcement as well."

"Oh that's right," Karena said. "I'm sorry, Mom. I forgot all about that. Go ahead, what's your announcement?"

"I have a new job," Noreen said without preamble.

"A job? Doing what?" Monica asked.

"Well, you remember when you and Sam came back from Brazil and you told me about those street children."

Karena smiled and nodded. "Go on."

"I did some research and found what you said was absolutely true. So I started thinking about it and I wrote up a proposal. I called Beverly Donovan and ran the idea past her and, well, we've started a new foundation."

"You and the Donovans have started a foundation? Together?" Deena asked, swallowing the lump in her throat.

"Yes. Beverly and her sister-in-law, Alma. They both thought it was a wonderful idea. We've been having conference calls and they both came out here over the summer to meet with me. We're kicking it off with a big gala two weeks after New Year's. It'll take place in Las Vegas but the headquarters will be here in New York. I'll be running it."

"Wow," was Karena's response. "I am so proud of you, Mama. So very proud." Karena had come from around the table and hugged her mother.

Deena was almost speechless. Coming to this brunch today just wasn't a good idea. At every turn she was being reminded of Max. "I'm proud of you too, Mama," she said finally, getting up and hugging her mother just like Karena did.

Monica was last to get up, kissing Noreen on the cheek then hugging her. "It's going to be a huge success because you're behind it. I can't wait until it gets off the ground."

Deena couldn't wait to get home. Her head was spinning—no, it was starting to throb. She wanted to get up and leave but that would cause too many questions. Once again, she couldn't break down, couldn't be free to feel whatever she was feeling. It just wasn't like her, not in their eyes.

When she was back in her apartment Deena let out a sigh of relief. Today had been eventful. All the information she'd received from a three-hour visit with her mother and sisters was a lot for her to digest.

Karena was getting married to the wonderful love of her life, Sam. Her mother was beside herself with excitement to be working side by side with Beverly and Alma Donovan on a charity to help save the street children in South America. Beyond the wedding news, mention of the Donovan name made Deena edgy. Alma Donovan was Max's mother. Her mother was working on a charity benefit to be held in approximately three weeks in Las Vegas kicking off their joint venture. Of course, Noreen wanted all of her children there. Monica had already claimed a business trip she couldn't get out of. Karena was going to speak to Sam about them both traveling out together and maybe speaking to Camille about designing her wedding dress. That left Deena.

Was she going to go or was she going to be chicken and remain in New York? If her mother wanted her there, it stood to reason that Alma Donovan would want her son there as well. Could she face seeing him again after he'd so easily brushed her off?

Of course she could. After all, she wasn't some simpering teenage girl wearing her broken heart on her sleeve. She was a grown woman who had other options besides Max Donovan, especially if he was too blind to realize when he'd had a good thing.

It was with that attitude that Deena punched the buttons on her phone to replay the voice mail messages she'd received while she was out. There were only two and they were both from Kevin Langley, a literary agent who she'd spoken to a few months ago about representation. Since then she'd chosen and signed with an agent and was a bit surprised to hear Kevin's messages to call him back.

Dropping down onto her couch she replayed the last message, writing Kevin's number down as she did. Her fingers tapped restlessly on her knee while the phone rang after she'd dialed. She was thinking of what she was going to do for the rest of the day—whatever it was the plan did not consist of more pining over Max Donovan. That episode had to be over and done with as far as she was concerned. She'd wasted enough time on that man.

"Hi, Mr. Langley. This is Deena Lakefield, returning your call," she spoke into the phone after he'd answered.

"Hi, Deena. I was hoping you'd get back to me."

"No problem. I'm wondering if you received the email I sent you a few weeks ago that stated I'd signed with another agent and thanking you for your time."

"I did. Very professional of you. I'm sorry we couldn't have the chance to work together. But that gives me the opportunity to ask the question I really wanted to ask when we met."

She remembered their meeting. They'd had lunch in late September. She'd been distracted, still thinking about her trip to Hilton Head, but realizing that her career needed her attention. Kevin had been very knowledgeable about the romance industry, naming a few of his more successful clients as well as editors he had connections with. He would have been perfect for her, except Eliza Jackson was better, and she loved Deena's writing. It was so important to have people who really got her work, it made it so much easier to sell the finished product.

"Oh. And what question was that?" she asked, wanting to know why he was still contacting her.

"Would you have dinner with me?"

Deena was rarely caught speechless. She was too mouthy and too opinionated, her family said. Still, at this moment she didn't know what to say. Usually when a man was hitting on her she knew it and would either flirt right back or make it clear that she wasn't interested. This she hadn't seen coming. Maybe because she'd been really preoccupied when she'd first met Kevin. She'd fancied herself in love and was waiting for the continuation of the most intense relationship she'd ever experienced.

Well, that was then.

"Ah, sure. That sounds like a nice idea. Just let me know when and where."

"Is tonight too soon?" he asked with a slight chuckle.

She was shaking her head as she spoke. "No. Tonight is perfect."

She'd resolved to get over Max Donovan. There was no time like the present to get started with that goal.

Chapter 7

Las Vegas, Nevada

Max rubbed his fingers over the smooth surface of the seashell. Sitting in his office alone, staring out the window, his thoughts wandered. It was the day after Christmas and he was in the office, early. He should have been home or at his parents', having breakfast, still celebrating the holidays. But he wasn't in the mood.

There wasn't a day that she hadn't crossed his mind. Her smile. Her laugh. Her voice when she moaned his name. He felt like moaning himself, in misery. She was everything he'd ever wanted in a woman, everything he thought he needed. And yet she was unreachable.

Sure, he had her home phone number, her cell, her email, her snail mail address. But he couldn't contact her, couldn't reach out and grab what he wanted. Again.

He should be used to it by now. Still, it stung. The knowledge that he was doing the right thing, giving Deena Lakefield the life she truly deserved, failed to soothe the incessant ache.

Glancing down at the seashell he smiled. The fact that Sandy Pines was just about ready for its grand reopening didn't help a bit. He'd kept in contact with Dalila as well as the crews he'd hired to do the remodeling of the property. Things were going well. In fact, it was past time he returned to have a look at the work. One woman, who lived in New York City, held him back. Traveling to the East Coast wasn't appealing to Max unless he was planning to see her. That he adamantly refused to do.

She had another book coming out in a couple of months. The one she was working on when they were in Hilton Head. He wondered if it were about them, if he would read it. Instinct said he would, emotion said he shouldn't.

"Why are you here?" Ben walked in with his slow swagger and easy smile.

He was younger than Max by two years and by far the more personable brother. Max tended to be more solitary and nonchalant than Ben's open friendliness. And while Max had his father's serious and reserved nature, Ben definitely had their mother's boisterous and friendly personality.

"I could ask you the same thing," was Max's reply. He turned in his chair so that he was now facing Ben, tossing the seashell back into the bag it had been delivered in.

"Cool, what's this? Another Christmas gift?"

Ben was digging inside the box before Max could

stop him. In one hand he held the update letter from Dalila and in the other a couple of the seashells she'd sent. The seashells were ones he and Deena had collected one day on the beach. Apparently they'd both left them when they packed to come home. In her letter Dalila said she'd just found them. Max assumed she'd sent half to Deena and the other half to him. In the letter she'd also included her advice on his relationship with Deena. It was nothing she hadn't said to him before. Nothing he probably hadn't said to himself at some point. But none of it made a difference.

"Would it matter if I said it was personal?"

Ben shrugged, already looking down at the letter. "Nah."

He was going to have something to say. Max knew this like he knew today's date. Ben always had something to say about everything. It just was not in his nature to keep his thoughts or opinions to himself. This made it hard whenever they were trying to pull something over on their parents during their younger years. Ben wasn't good at keeping secrets either.

"Who's Dalila and why is she giving you advice on your love life? 'Come see ein like come stay.' That doesn't even sound like good English." He frowned, reciting from the letter. "Sounds a little old for your taste in women."

"Sounds personal to me," Max said, looking at his computer screen that had a blank email box open. One line, that's what he'd send her, a Merry Christmas wish.

"It's postmarked South Carolina. Does this someone have to do with Mom's project? She's really excited about that, you know. She's talking about all of us taking a trip there this summer. But I think she expects you to go a little sooner, bring her back some good news maybe."

"There's no need for me to go back. The crew have been sending pictures so I know everything's going along fine."

"But you always do a personal walk-through before declaring the project finished."

"I did the beginning work. Adam can close up the deal. Camille and the baby are doing just fine. Maybe all three of them can take the trip." Josiah Randolph Donovan, who had been named after Camille's late father, was Adam's son, born in late September, right on time and healthy as can be. Camille and Adam adored their son so it was rare that you would see either one of them without him being close by.

"But it's Mom's place."

Max sighed. "What do you want, Ben? I know you didn't come all the way to my office to see me and tell me what Mom wants."

"I want to know what's been eating at you lately. Well, not just me, but the entire family. Adam says you've been like an ogre to work with. Aunt Beverly says you haven't been to her house for dinner in weeks. And you know that's unlike you. Adam and Linc say it's a woman. I'm thinking not because my big brother never lets a lady stress him."

Ben had taken a seat and now folded one leg over the other at the knee. He rubbed a finger over the freshly cut goatee at his chin. "Or have you finally taken the plunge like the other Donovan men before you?"

Max frowned. "You know better than to ask a question that stupid. No, I haven't taken the plunge. I don't ever intend to take that trip, thank you."

Ben chuckled. "That's what the others said."

"I'm not them. And you of all people should know that."

"Hey." Ben shrugged. "All I know is you've been real cranky and we're getting tired of it. So if it's a woman, find her, sleep with her, do whatever you have to do, just get it done so things can go back to normal."

"I don't know what you're talking about. Things are as normal as they're likely to be for me."

For a moment Ben was quiet and Max knew that meant trouble.

"Is this about your medical condition?"

"Drop it, Ben." He pushed away from his desk and stood, going to the window to stare out at absolutely nothing.

"It is. Come on, Max, you know nothing's definite. Doctors are coming up with new cures all the time. You can go back, get tested again."

"Be disappointed again. No, thank you. Just forget it, Ben. I'm handling it."

"You're not handling it, you're settling. And it's starting to piss me off."

Max turned to face his brother who had gotten up to come stand beside him. "Then you can get out of my office!"

"Look, what happened to you was crappy. The diagnosis totally sucks, but there are ways to get around it. Ways that don't consist of you trying to make a monk out of yourself."

"I don't have anything against women and you know that."

"But you have something against commitment. Is that what's going on? Some woman touched something in you, something beyond the physical and now you're all bent out of shape because you can't make kids?"

Before he could think better of it Max had grabbed Ben by the front of his shirt, pushing him back against the wall. "Don't push me, Ben. Just don't."

"Brute strength doesn't change the truth," his younger brother said, looking him straight in the eye. "You can't fix the problem this way."

Disgusted with himself for reacting to his brother's words, Max snatched his hands away from Ben, taking a couple steps back. He took a deep breath then let it out. "It's not that simple, Ben. It's just not that easy to say, hey, this is the hand I've been dealt and move on. Getting involved, seriously involved with a woman would require me to be honest with her, to tell her that I'm less than a man."

"That's bull! The fact that you're sterile has nothing to do with your manhood. That's a state of mind, a maturity that you exude. Remember Dad telling us that when we were teenagers."

Rubbing his hands down his face, Max sighed again. "Yeah, I remember it. I know what you're saying is true, but it's just not that easy."

"So you did meet a woman that has you thinking about telling her the truth? Who is she? Do I know her?"

"You don't know her and I'm not going to see her again. It's for the best."

"For you or her? If you ask me, I think you should let people make up their own minds. Tell her and see what she says. If she walks, she wasn't worth it in the first place. If she sticks, then you've probably got a keeper."

"But it's not fair to keep her if I can't give her what she wants, what she needs."

With a nod of his head Ben moved toward the door. "If you don't at least tell her you'll never know what she's willing to accept. You can't make the decision for you *and* her. It's not fair and it's sort of cowardly."

Wisely, Ben opened and closed the door behind him, leaving Max alone after that parting remark. Max frowned because had his brother still been standing there he couldn't really say he wouldn't have jacked him up again.

No matter how wrong and immature he knew that would be.

There was some truth to Ben's words, Max knew this. But this wasn't Ben's fight. His younger brother's eternal optimism could not change the facts.

Max was sterile.

He would never be able to get a woman pregnant.

Deena Lakefield wanted a family, a husband and children.

How could he deny her that?

Chapter 8

He was on the East Coast, it would be rude not to at least stop by to see her. It had been rude not to call her in the last six months. She'd called him, those first few weeks after Hilton Head. She'd called, texted and emailed. He listened to messages, read texts and emails. But he hadn't returned the courtesy. He'd been, just like Ben accused, a coward.

It was ridiculous, no reason why they couldn't be friends, even if there was no future between them intimately.

So he'd wrapped up his three-day inspection of the resort in Hilton Head and booked a flight up the coast to New York. He wasn't staying, just wanted to stop by and see her, say hello, then he would be on another flight home. The mounting guilt he'd felt for the way he handled things between them would be assuaged and he could get on with his life.

But fate wasn't on his side.

"If she hasn't answered by now, she's not there," a female voice said from behind him.

Max had been standing in the lobby of an upscale apartment building just around the corner from New York's Central Park. He'd been ringing the buzzer identified with Deena's name for about ten or fifteen minutes, but he really wasn't keeping time. Turning around, he was hoping to see a friendly neighbor who might be able to offer some ideas of where Deena might be. Instead he saw her.

Hands down she was one very attractive woman. She was dressed in a charcoal-gray pantsuit and wearing heels that put her eye level with him. Max could tell she was a viable opponent for any man.

"Hello. I'm Maxwell Donovan," he said, extending a hand to her.

She raised an elegantly arched brow and glanced at his hand. After a moment's hesitation she extended her own, allowed him to shake it. "You're looking for Deena Lakefield?"

"Yes. Do you know her?" He had a feeling she did, why else would she come up and speak to him about ringing Deena's buzzer?

"I may. The question is, does she know you?"

Yeah, she definitely knew Deena and was more than a little protective of her. He wondered if they were related. "Yes, she does. We haven't seen each other in a while. I was in town and decided to pay her a visit."

She nodded, her expression changing as if she had some secret he didn't know. "Well, she's not here."

"Can I leave a message with you for her?" He knew the answer before he'd finished the question. This woman did not like him, which Max found odd since she didn't know him. Still, he was getting a definite dislike vibe.

"I'm not a messenger."

He nodded. "Okay. Well, just in case you happen to see her or talk to her you can mention that I stopped by."

"That would be giving her a message, now wouldn't it? Maybe you should wait until she comes home."

The last remark didn't seem like a genuine offer, more like some type of trap. Max didn't know what to think of this woman. And he didn't have time to find out. His flight home was leaving in an hour and a half. He had just enough time to get out of the city and to the airport without having to chase the plane down the tarmac.

"I don't have time," he replied. "If you see her and you feel like delivering the message, I'd appreciate it."

He moved past her, heading toward the door.

"And if I don't feel like giving her the message?" the woman asked from behind him.

He didn't know what was up with her, but was supremely glad he didn't have to deal with her on a regular basis. "Then I guess she won't get it," was his comeback as he pushed through the door and left her standing there.

January—Las Vegas, Nevada

"As godfather, you should be prepared to pick up where the parents leave off. If they fail to bring this child up in the way of the Lord, it is your responsibility to do so," Pastor Danté Miles said with his normal candor and seriousness.

Max nodded his head, agreeing to the pastor's words, feeling his heart swell with love for the tiny bundle being held in his arms.

Josiah Randolph Donovan stared up at him with Camille's wide brown eyes and Adam's smiling mouth. The baby wiggled and Max tightened his grip, making sure he held him securely. This wasn't the first time he'd held this little guy. No, he'd been one of the first to arrive at the hospital late that night in September when Adam called to say he was rushing Camille to the hospital. And at Adam's urging he'd been one of the first in the room after Camille had delivered, holding a groggy eight-pound, three-ounce baby in his arms. Adam had asked him to be the godfather as he'd stood in the hospital waiting room later that evening. Tears pricked the back of his eyes then, as they did now, months later.

Behind him most of the Donovan family stood— Camille and Adam to his one side, Camille's best friend and Josiah's godmother, Dana Palmer, on his other. The service of dedication was almost over. Afterward, they would leave the church and head straight to Camille and Adam's house for Sunday dinner. This would be the first time he'd been around the entire family in weeks. He only hoped the focus could remain on Josiah, Adam and Camille and not on why he hadn't been around.

Unfortunately, he had no such luck.

An hour later they were in Adam's den, Adam, Linc, Trent, Brock and Ben. He was technically in front of the firing squad. Brock and Noelle had come out from

Maryland for this special event, but just because his cousin and his future wife didn't live on the West Coast, didn't mean they didn't know everything that was going on out here. Brock sat on the couch holding a bottle of beer in his hand. Linc and Adam were seated at the bar while Trent stood near the window. Ben was in a recliner shaking his glass until the ice cubes clinked, signifying he needed another drink.

"So you want to tell us what's going on?" Linc began.

Out of this group of Donovans, Linc was the oldest. That gave him an air of authority that Max didn't feel like dealing with today.

"Nothing," he said in a clipped tone, casting an irritated glare at Ben. He felt like strangling his younger brother, but knew that would only lead to more inquiries.

"Bull!" Ben spoke up quickly. He'd ignored Max's glare and was moving to the bar to get another drink.

"You really need to mind your own business," Max answered his brother's remark.

"Since when are you not our business?" This was Trent, the private investigator, ex–Navy SEAL, the strong arm of the family.

But Max wasn't afraid. "Since I'm a grown man capable of dealing with whatever is going on in my life on my own."

"We're only trying to help, man. No need to get all snippy with us," Adam added.

Max ran a hand down his face and took a deep breath. He was not in the mood for this. "I'm fine."

"You look exhausted. You're working late hours, not showing up for brunch or basketball or golf, or anything else we get together to do. You were like a zombie at your parents' on Christmas and now you're here looking like you've lost your best friend," Linc recapped. "I'd say you're anything but fine."

"It's not that big a deal. Just let it go," Max said.

"You were right, Linc. It's a woman." Trent grinned.

Brock took a swallow of his beer. "Really? You're this cranky over a woman? Who is she? I've got to meet the woman that could tie you in knots."

Max glared at him. "I am not tied in knots. You're all just blowing this out of proportion. So what if I haven't been around a lot? I do have a life, you know."

Adam nodded. "You do. But normally your family's a big part of that life. You're shutting us out, man. And we're just trying to figure out why."

"Because while you may be content to do without us until this little storm blows over, we feel inclined to help you out. Call us crazy, but that's what families usually do."

This was Linc again, a calm voice of authority in a room full of volatile men.

"I looked up this Dalila woman from Hilton Head. I know you're not pining over a sixty-year-old Gullah woman with more wisdom than money who cooks food that tastes like heaven."

"Damn it, Trent! When are you going to learn you can't just run background checks on everybody you meet?" Max roared.

Trent shrugged. "I'm a licensed P.I. I can run background checks on anyone I damn well please. Especially if it's going to help a stubborn, no-brained family member."

Max grit his teeth so hard he might need to pay a

visit to his dentist before the week was out. "Dalila has nothing to do with this."

"I figured as much. Still she's our only link to whatever happened to you in Hilton Head. The moment you came back you were acting strange and now months later you're still not back to normal," Ben said.

"Your normal," Max tossed back. "Who's to say a guy can't change? So what if I want to work more, stay to myself more. What's the harm in that?"

"The harm is," Brock stated, leaning forward to place his empty bottle on the end table, "that staying to yourself isn't going to make the problem go away. Believe me, I know what I'm talking about."

Max didn't dispute that. Brock had spent much of his adulthood alone in Maryland, having opted to move away from his father and twin sister and brother in Dallas. And because of the scandal that followed his birth parents he'd felt resigned to the life of a loner. Until Noelle Vincent came along. Now, Brock was at every family function he could make it out here for, with a smiling Noelle and her huge diamond engagement ring right beside him.

"It was just a fling," Max said finally. "Just a summer affair that ended when we both returned to our respective homes. That's all."

Every man in the room looked at him, waiting. Max hated the silence, hated that they expected him to say something, or that they were about to say something else.

"Have you talked to her since then?" Linc asked.

"No."

"Did you call her?" This was Adam's question.

"No."

From Linc, "Did she call you?"

"Yes."

Trent raised a brow. "How many times?"

Max cleared his throat. "Four."

Ben made a whistling sound. "And you just ignored her?"

"I thought it was best."

"For who?" Linc asked.

"Her," he said then swore. "Both of us."

"I get it, you aren't right for each other. And you don't think it would work out. So you should have just told her that, not ignored her," Brock stated.

"It wasn't like that. I mean, she was a really nice woman. A bit on the young side, but still nice. And we had a good time together. It just couldn't go any further."

"What does that mean, 'on the young side'?" Trent asked suspiciously.

"Not like that. She's twenty-nine."

"Good, she's legal," Ben said with a grin. "Is she married?"

"You know better than that. I don't do married women. She's a nice girl, from a good family. She writes books and she was fun to be with. But it's over and so is this conversation."

He headed to the door, stopped just before putting his hand on the knob. "Look, fellas," he said then turned back to face his brother and cousins. "I really appreciate your support but this is just something I'm going to have to deal with on my own. And don't worry, I'll deal with it. It's just taking a little longer than I expected to move on. At any rate, everything will be fine. And I'll be at the next basketball game, just name the time and place."

The second Max was through the door, closing it quietly behind him, the remaining Donovan men looked at each other.

"I told you," Ben said. "He's got it bad."

Brock nodded. "Yeah, he does."

"He's just too damned stubborn to see it." Trent chuckled. "I wonder where he gets that from."

Linc rubbed a hand over his goatee. "It's hereditary and you know it. Still, I think Max is carrying a little more than just Donovan stubbornness with him."

"He is," Ben agreed. "He thinks by staying away from this woman he's doing her a favor. You know, because of his condition."

"Damn," Trent swore. "I forgot all about that."

"That's crazy. There's nothing wrong with Max. He can function sexually. I know, just ask the night supervisor at the Gramercy," Linc said.

"What? Max and one of your employees?" Ben asked.

"Yeah. It was last year, but she couldn't stop talking about it. At least not until I told her if I heard one more word about her night with my cousin in one of my hotel rooms, while she was on the clock, she was going to be fired."

Trent shook his head. "Good ole Max."

"But just because he can perform the task doesn't mean he can do the deed. Maybe this woman told him she wants children," Brock added.

"Damn, he was only in Hilton Head for one month. She wanted a child that fast?" Trent queried.

Ben finished his drink and placed his glass on the bar. "She didn't ask to have his baby. He just feels like he's cheating her out of a full relationship if he stays with her."

Trent made an indistinguishable noise. "Wish I knew her name."

"Why?" Brock asked. "You gonna do another background check?"

Trent shrugged. "Might."

"That's not going to help," Linc said finally. "I think Max might be right this time. This might be an issue only he can work through. No matter how good our intentions are."

"Then we're all in for a long time of watching him sulk," Ben said.

"God, I hope not. I hate seeing a man look so pitiful."

"Good thing I'm going home tomorrow," Brock said with a smile.

"Good thing there's such a thing as conference calls, and if need be private jets to bring us right to your doorstep for some much needed relief," Linc said.

Ben stared at the door his brother had just walked out of. "Yeah, we might need that. Soon."

Chapter 9

New York

"How long will you be gone?" Kevin asked as they stood at the check-in line at the airport.

He held her luggage and her carry-on bag. Deena had her purse and an uneasy feeling in the pit of her stomach.

"Just the weekend. The party is on Saturday night. I'm going early with my parents so I can be there with my mother for support."

"That's very nice of you. Are your sisters going?"

"Karena and Sam might fly in Saturday morning. Sam was working on a big case and Karena was waiting for a shipment today. Monica can't come."

"So it's just you and your parents?"

"Yes," she answered but she sensed there was something more to his question.

Kevin was a really nice guy—thirty years old, five foot eleven, medium brown skin tone and deep brown eyes. In the short time she'd known him she'd surmised he was detail-oriented and attentive to both his clients and to her. There really was no reason not to like him. Except that she couldn't get her mind off another man.

The fact that the other man was a total jackass didn't really make it better. Max Donovan was a bona fide idiot and she was tired of trying to rationalize what she was feeling for him. It was time she really started the road to getting over him. But she wasn't sure that road included a side trip with Kevin.

"Well, I guess this is it." Deena had never had a guy walk her all the way into the airport and stand in the check-in line with her. Once she was past check-in only ticketed passengers could go the rest of the way. For some reason she was glad about that.

In the three weeks since she'd first gone out with Kevin he'd seemed to be everywhere she was. Not like a stalker or anything but, whenever they were on a date, he was pulling out her chair, walking her to the ladies' room, offering to carry everything from her purse to her tray of food when they'd stopped at Burger King after a late movie one night. He called her every morning before she was up and ready to go to the gym. He called her at midday to see if she was writing and then they saw each other in the evenings. It sounded like a lot but Deena thought it might be very therapeutic. If she was talking to Kevin and being with Kevin she wouldn't have time to think about Max. Unfortunately, it wasn't quite working out that way.

"So I'll see you when I get back," she said after she'd

gotten her boarding pass. She reached for her bags, but instead was pulled into Kevin's embrace.

His lips were familiar now, warm and subtly attractive. When they met hers she gave a light peck. But Kevin wanted more. He pressed against her harder, pushing his tongue against her lips. Deena was no stranger to public displays of affection; however, she was a bit too old to be sharing such an intimate kiss in the middle of the airport. She loosened up slightly, kissed him again without parting her lips then pulled away.

"Miss me," he said in a tone that almost sounded desperate.

"Sure," she said and hurriedly took her suitcase and bag from him. She didn't waste a moment turning and walking away, heading toward the gate like her plane was about to pull out.

Not once did she look back so she had no idea if Kevin stood there staring at her walk away. She suspected he had, but didn't want to see it personally.

On the plane an hour later Deena let her mind wander. She was going to Las Vegas, to a party being hosted by two Donovan women and her mother. They were kicking off the Karing for Kidz Foundation, a program to help support the street children of South America as well as the orphanages in the United States. This was her mother's debut into the philanthropic world and Deena wanted to be by her side to support her, the way her mother had always tried to do for her.

Her father wasn't thrilled, but he was going to be there. He'd changed since the getaway the two of them had taken last year, mellowing out a bit about the things Noreen was supposed to be doing with her life. He'd

KIMANI ™
ROMANCE

An Important Message from the Publisher

Dear Reader,

Because you've chosen to read one of our fine novels, I'd like to say "thank you"! And, as a special way to say thank you, I'm offering to send you two more Kimani™ Romance novels and two surprise gifts— absolutely FREE! These books will keep it real with true-to-life African American characters that turn up the heat and sizzle with passion.

Please enjoy the free books and gifts with our compliments...

Glenda Howard

For Kimani Press™

Peel off Seal and Place Inside...

EDITOR'S
FREE GIFTS
SEAL
THANK YOU

K-ROM-11B

W e'd like to send you two free books to introduce you to Kimani™ Romance books. These novels feature strong, sexy women, and African-American heroes that are charming, loving and true. Our authors fill each page with exceptional dialogue, exciting plot twists, and enough sizzling romance to keep you riveted until the very end!

KIMANI ROMANCE...LOVE'S ULTIMATE DESTINATION

Your two books have combined cover price of $12.50 in the U.S. $14.50 in Canada, bu are yours **FREE!**

We'll even send you two wonderful surprise gifts. You can't lose!

THE EDITOR'S "THANK YOU" FREE GIFTS INCLUDE:

➤ Two Kimani™ Romance Novels
➤ Two exciting surprise gifts

YES! I have placed my Editor's "thank you" Free Gifts seal in the space provided at right. Please send me 2 FREE books, and my 2 FREE Mystery Gifts. I understand that I am under no obligation to purchase anything further, as explained on the back of this card.

PLACE
FREE GIFTS
SEAL
HERE

168/368 XDL FEJY

Please Print

FIRST NAME

LAST NAME

ADDRESS

APT.#   CITY

STATE/PROV.   ZIP/POSTAL CODE

Thank You!

▲ Detach card and mail today. No stamp needed. ▲

The Reader Service - Here's How It Works:

even eased up a bit on his daughters, accepting that God had blessed him with girls instead of boys. As for the way Paul Lakefield treated Deena, he still wasn't happy with her career choice. He just didn't voice it as much. Thank goodness. The last thing she needed right now was her father's criticism. One man driving her insane was enough.

"You want to tell me what's going on with you, young lady?" Noreen Lakefield asked with her slight Southern accent.

Deena took a deep breath and tried to get herself together before turning from the window to face her mother. She'd been thinking about him again, about what could have possibly gone wrong. It was stupid, she knew. She should just let it go, that was the smart thing. But sometimes the heart just wasn't smart enough.

"I'm fine. We should get going. You don't want to be late for your first fundraiser," she said, turning quickly and moving right past her mother, headed toward the door.

"If there's one thing I will not stand for it's a child that I gave birth to lying to my face. Now, I'm going to ask you one more time, but mind you, it's really not a question that you have a choice in answering. What's the matter with you?"

It was the no-nonsense sound of her voice, or maybe the high altitude—they were on the twenty-third floor of this hotel—or maybe it was just that she was tired of carrying this burden. Whatever the real reason, Deena found herself turning from the door and dropping down onto the couch in the center of the living room portion of the suite, spilling everything.

"I met this guy in Hilton Head. He was really nice and I thought we hit it off. He didn't call. He didn't return my calls or my emails. Nothing. I know what you're going to say, I should get over him. I'm such an idiot for jumping into bed with him. You're going to say you told me to be careful, to make better choices. I know and really I've tried. I'm even dating someone else but this other guy's in my head and I can't get him out. I don't know why and it's driving me insane."

"First," Noreen said, moving with slow, regal movements to sit on the couch beside her youngest child. "Don't presume to tell me what I'm going to say. I don't know why you and your sisters insist on thinking you were born with ESP. Furthermore, dating somebody else isn't going to erase the feelings you have for another man. That's just foolishness. You have to deal with those feelings head-on."

"What? How?"

"When he didn't call you or answer you, you should have gone to see him, made him tell you what was going on face-to-face."

"Wouldn't that be chasing him?"

"No, that would be making him stand up and be a man about why he doesn't want to see you anymore."

"Probably because I'm a scatterbrained writer."

"You are not scatterbrained," Noreen said, using a finger to tap on Deena's head. "You're an intelligent, beautiful woman with a lot to offer the right man. And, baby, if he's not running, skipping and jumping through hoops to claim you then he's not the right man."

Deena sighed, sinking back into the chair. "I thought he could be."

"Oh, my little Deena. You've got such a big heart and

so much love to give to someone, someday. You don't have to rush it, you're still young."

"But it hurts right here, Mama," she said, clutching a fist to her chest.

Noreen wanted to sigh right along with her. If her baby was hurting, so was she. And if Deena, the most vivacious and outgoing of her children, was suffering then this man must really be something.

"Why don't you go and see him? For all you know something could have happened to him."

"No, I don't think so. At least I hope he's all right. I just don't know what to do. And now there's Kevin."

"Kevin's the one you're seeing now?"

Deena nodded.

"But he's not the one you want?"

She shook her head.

"Why you young people make things so difficult I'll never understand. When I first saw your father I just knew I wanted that man. My sisters told me he was too rich, too cultured to want an ole country gal like me. But I was determined that when that man left Beaufort I was going with him."

"Really?" Deena perked up a little, interested in how her parents had met and courted each other. "What'd you do?"

"Girl, I put on my best clothes and hot-combed my hair, styling it with nice tight curls. I put on lipstick and I went to him."

"Oh my goodness, Mama, you threw yourself at Daddy?"

"Not threw myself, child. I presented him an offer."

Noreen batted her eyelashes and they both laughed.

"An offer he couldn't refuse, huh?" Deena asked.

"Something like that. The point is, baby, that I saw something I wanted and I went after it. Now, if at any time your father would have opened his mouth and told me to get lost, I would have done it. With my head held high and a sway in my hips that he would have never forgotten."

Deena laughed again. "I'll just bet you would have."

"Go to this man and ask him what's going on. If he doesn't want you, fine. He's not worth the air you breathe. But if he's man enough to capture your heart, I think he might have a lick of sense and he might just use it when he sees you."

"I don't know, seems like begging to me."

"You young folks," Noreen said for what seemed to Deena like the billionth time. "It's a confrontation. You want him to be big enough to turn you down to your face, then you have to have guts enough to get in his face."

And this was the woman Karena thought didn't have a backbone. Noreen Lakefield had more knowledge and more courage than any woman Deena had ever known.

"I love you, Mama."

She threw her arms around her mother and squeezed tight.

Patting her back, Noreen smiled and said, "I love you, too, baby. Now, go find that young man and set him straight."

Chapter 10

An hour later Deena walked into the grand ballroom at the Gramercy Casino on the strip of Las Vegas.

From what she'd seen so far—from the main entrance, through the long golden hallways, up the elevator and into the large and lavishly decorated grand ballroom— the Gramercy was a beautiful hotel. It was also a casino, that she noted from the discreet signs throughout the main entrance and on the elevators directing guests to the west wing of the building for gaming entertainment. Normally Deena loved to gamble, not necessarily for the money, but for the adrenaline rush. She was actually pretty good at poker without even trying. But she hadn't had the time to indulge in a while. Maybe she would tonight after the festivities.

She'd arrived with her parents, they were arm in arm and she stood right beside her mother.

"This is my youngest daughter, Deena," her mother introduced her.

Deena smiled and shook the hands of both of the lovely women standing in front of her.

"I'm Beverly Donovan," the taller one with shoulder-length dark curls said first. She was beautiful, looking like she could be in her early forties instead of a mother and grandmother.

"And I'm Alma Donovan," the other woman said.

She, Deena thought with a pang in her chest, looked just like her son. Alma Donovan was a shade or two darker than Max, but the eyes were the same, a mystical kind of color that at first glance wasn't positively green or gray. Max's she knew now, after glancing at them in the sunlight and in the moonlight and in the wee hours of the morning, were undeniably green. Alma's were fastened to Deena as if she'd seen her someplace before.

"It's a pleasure to meet you both." Deena cleared her throat and spoke finally. "My mother has spoken very highly of you and your endeavors."

"Your mother is a gem," Beverly said. "We're so happy we could get together and do this. It's such a worthy cause."

Alma was still smiling at Deena. "You're absolutely right, Beverly. Helping the children in need is more than a worthy cause. Do you have a husband and children, Deena?"

Wow, and Deena thought she was the candid one. "Ah, no, not yet."

"Deena's a writer," Noreen offered. "Her first book was released about nine months ago."

"Oh really? How nice. I've never met a real live writer before," Beverly said. "What do you write?"

"Romance," Deena said proudly.

"Black love," Alma said, shaking her head. "There's nothing like it."

Noreen reached for Paul's hand. "Nothing at all."

Deena Lakefield was a pretty young lady with a bright smile and intelligent eyes. She was, in Alma's quick assessment, perfect for Ben.

"Come, Deena. As a matter of fact, I think there are a few people here from the publishing industry. Now would be a great time for you to meet them."

"Sure," Deena said, eagerly breaking away from the crowd to walk along with Mrs. Donovan.

The older woman had threaded her arm through Deena's as they began to walk. "I'm so proud to know a published author. And to think I've been working closely with your mother all these months and had no clue. You know we're practically family now," Alma was saying.

Deena groaned inwardly. They could have legally been family if her son was even remotely interested in her.

"I'm really proud of what you and my mother have built here. I think Karing Kidz will be a huge success for both families."

"I do, too. Beverly and I always wanted to do something specifically for the children. It's our hope to take this global. Starting with North and South American children in need was almost mandated since our families are connected to both areas."

"Really? You have family in South America?" Deena asked. They were almost to the other side of the ballroom, near the buffets and the bar.

"Well, sort of indirectly. My nephew Trent is in partnership with a Sam Desdune on the East Coast."

Deena nodded. "I know Sam. He's engaged to my sister."

"Really? Wow, this is definitely a small world. Then you know that Sam's sister is married to Lorenzo Bennett, who is the son of Marvin and Beatriz Bennett. Beatriz is originally from Brazil."

Deena remembered very well. "Sam and Karena went to Pirata last year. They stayed with a princess and prince there."

Now Alma was nodding. "You're exactly right. It was through them that we found out about the street children in Brazil and the man trying to help them with limited funds. That really sparked our interest. Your mother was actually the first to make contact with that man and then she called us. So you see what I mean—we're family indirectly."

The older woman chuckled and Deena found herself relaxing. It was like being with her own mother. When they arrived at the bar Alma requested two flutes of champagne and just as they were about to take their first sip Deena saw her signal for someone. In the next minute a man was standing with them.

He was tall with an athletic build, his complexion a dark brown, his eyes a lighter shade of the same color. His smile was easy, that was a relief to her and when he extended his hand in greeting she found herself eager to respond.

"This is my son, Benjamin. Ben, this is Deena Lakefield."

Her son? Max's brother?

"Oh, if you'll excuse me, I see someone I must speak

with." And just like that Alma was gone and Deena was alone with Ben.

"Could she have been any less subtle?" Ben asked, slipping a hand into his pocket.

Deena laughed. "I was thinking that but wasn't going to say it."

"It's okay, she means well. So your parents are in partnership with mine?"

"Looks that way," was her reply.

"Then we should definitely toast to new beginnings," he said, scooping a champagne flute from the bar and lifting it in her direction.

"You are absolutely right," Deena said smiling and lifting her glass to clink against his. "New beginnings."

"You clean up well," Jade said, coming to her tiptoes to kiss Max on his cheek.

"Gee, thanks," he responded, smiling at his cousin's wife. A woman who had become like a sister to him. "You look exceptionally gorgeous yourself. Linc isn't half as smart as I thought he was, letting you come to this party all by yourself."

A strong clap on his back greeted those words and Max winked at Jade.

"Get your own woman and stop hitting on my wife," Linc taunted.

"Stop leaving her alone and vulnerable," Max said turning to shake his cousin's hand.

"This room is full of Donovan men. Any other man would have to be out of his mind to try to poach on my territory here."

"Did you forget who you were referring to?" Trent

Donovan said, joining the small crowd. "What's up, cousin? Haven't seen you in a while."

"I've been busy," Max spoke in his own defense.

"So I've heard," Trent said.

"And where's your wife? You in the habit of leaving her alone too?"

"No man in his right mind, period, would make a play for my wife. They know they'd have me to contend with," Trent said with a confident smile. "She's on a photo shoot in L.A."

"It must be a task having to keep tabs on a wife and stay in shape to keep poachers away from her," he said. It was meant as a thought, but he'd spoken it aloud.

"Your time's coming," Jade spoke up, giving him a knowing look.

Max was already shaking his head. "Nah, I don't think so."

And he really didn't. Marriage was not something that he foresaw for himself. He'd dismissed that possibility a long time ago. But Max didn't want to think about that tonight. He just wanted to see his family, show his support to his mother and his aunt and go home.

Half an hour later, he was ready to do just that. His gaze had just scanned the room, socialites and more socialites were all he could see. He wanted to go home; tonight was not the night to be around people. He'd greeted all his family so there was no reason to stay. They'd say he came and stop nagging him about staying cooped up in his house. Turning away from the crowded ballroom Max was all set to make his departure when something caught his eye.

The color was bright, vibrant. The body was dangerous, sinful. The smile was…familiar.

She laughed, tossing her head back. Her hair, tight dark twists, was pulled up into some sort of bun with fat tendrils playing softly around her face. Her hands were on his shoulders, his were around her waist.

"Her" being Deena and "him" being Ben. His woman and his brother.

Rage moved through him like a swallow of bad beer. It was an acrid taste in his mouth and even as he swallowed he knew what was coming next wouldn't end well. Max was moving toward them long before he thought about where he was or who he was. All he could see was Ben's hands on Deena…Deena smiling up at Ben…Ben leering down at Deena in that form-fitting dress displaying everything he'd once touched, once kissed. His temples throbbed as he pushed through people in the crowd to get to his destination.

His fingers were already wrapping around the material of Ben's jacket, pulling him back away from Deena. Ben was already cursing, struggling to get out of Max's grip.

"Going from one brother to the next. I would have thought better of you, Deena."

For a minute she looked truly shocked—either that he was there or that he'd caught her flirting with his brother. Then that look quickly turned to anger.

"Are you out of your mind? Let him go!" she said, trying to keep her voice low.

"Why? So you can have your way with him next? I don't think so. He's leaving and so are you."

Max released Ben, casting him a heated glare. Then,

turning his attention back to Deena, he grabbed her by the wrist and proceeded to pull her through the crowd.

"Let me go, you big idiot!" she shouted from behind him, swinging her purse at his broad back.

Around him Max barely heard the audible gasps and murmurs of guests or saw the flicker of cameras. He was too focused on the woman that had been haunting his dreams for the past seven months and the brother he loved and trusted. How did they know each other? How long had whatever was going on between them been going on? He definitely did not appreciate being made a fool of.

"Max, what are you doing?" This was Trent, who had appeared in front of him, effectively blocking his path.

"You don't want to be in my way right now, man," was all Max said.

"I don't think you really want to be doing what you're doing, in this crowded room. What's going on? Who is she?"

Max pushed past Trent, declining to answer any more questions. Behind him Deena was hurling curses and struggling to break free. Her efforts were futile and only increased his anger.

"You're an insensitive jerk, you know that? I don't know why I ever thought I could be in love with you. Let me go!"

"Maxwell Frederick Donovan, what in the world are you doing?" That was his mother storming through the doors that led to the hallway where the back elevators were. His father was right beside her, a look of utter outrage on his face.

Even though they were away from all the guests,

Max and Deena still weren't alone. Every member of the Donovan clan that was at this party was now in this hallway. Along with two other people he didn't know, one, a man that was headed straight at him.

"Young man, you either release my daughter now or I'm going to—"

Alma touched a hand to the man's arm, then looked at Max.

"This is Ms. Lakefield's father. Now, I suggest you release his daughter before things get messier than I suspect they already are," she said in a serious tone.

Max's father, Everette Donovan, came up beside him. "Let her go, son."

Max felt his fingers releasing Deena's wrist a split second before he felt the palm of her hand connecting soundly with his right cheek.

"Don't you ever put your hands on me again!" she said before pushing past people and heading to the elevators.

The man, her father, followed her as well as the woman who had been with him. It was his guess that these were her parents, but what were they doing here? What was Deena doing here?

"What the hell's your problem?" Adam asked.

"He needs his head examined," Ben replied.

"You need to get your own woman and keep your hands off mine!" Max yelled at his brother.

"What?" It was a combined gasp from more than one person in the hallway so Max didn't know who to answer, not that he was really thinking of offering an answer.

In the short distance he heard the ding of the elevator arriving and looked over just in time to see Deena and her parents board. She stared right at him, rage simmering in thick rays across the space to spear him right in his heart.

"*Your* woman?" Trent asked.

Linc looked from the now closed elevator door to Max. "*That's* the woman from Hilton Head?"

With lips closed tight, Max simply nodded.

Ben threw back his head and laughed.

Adam was next to follow Ben's lead. Trent smiled but didn't let loose. And Linc, because he was older and supposedly wiser, just shook his head.

"You've got ten seconds to tell me what's going on, Max," Everette said in his booming voice. "And that's being generous. Your mother is giving you about two especially since you've made a spectacle at their first event and pissed off one of her partners."

"Partner? Who's your partner?" he asked his mother.

"If you would have acted like I'd taught you something about manners you would have been properly introduced to Mr. and Mrs. Paul Lakefield of the Lakefield Galleries in Manhattan. Noreen Lakefield has partnered with your aunt and myself in this new venture of ours."

The moment she said their names Max's stomach twisted. Damn it!

"Then what was *she* doing here?"

It was obvious to all of them who she was.

"She's their daughter. Their youngest daughter, who you just about dragged across the entire ballroom. Now, may I ask why?"

Max could do nothing but sigh. "Ask him," he said, nodding toward a still laughing Ben.

"I'm asking you," Alma said.

Swallowing what little bit of pride he had left, Max dutifully answered, "I met Deena Lakefield while I was in Hilton Head. She was staying at the Sandy Pines. We had…sort of had an affair. I haven't seen her since."

Everette's face was still grim, but Alma nodded as if she finally understood.

"This is why you've been in such a sour mood since you came back," she said knowingly.

"Nothing's wrong with my mood. Or at least it wasn't until I saw him all hugged up with Deena."

Ben held up his hands in mock surrender. "Bro, I just met her about ten minutes before you pulled the caveman routine."

"He's right. I just introduced them," Alma said. "Had you not been secretive all this time about the woman in your life I would have known not to try to set her up with one of my eligible sons. Why did you keep that from us?"

"She doesn't belong to me," Max muttered tightly.

"I can't tell," Trent spoke up.

Each of his cousins had a smirk on their faces, one Max wanted to wipe away with his anger.

"Just forget it," he said finally. "I'm sorry I ruined your evening," he said to his mother and walked toward the elevators.

"Max, I'm here if you want to talk about whatever is bothering you," Alma said, placing a hand on his shoulder.

With a heavy sigh he turned, pulled his mother into his arms and hugged her. "I know you are, Mom. But I'll be okay. I'll apologize to the Lakefields."

"That would be nice," Everette said then clapped a hand on his son's back. "If a woman can get that reaction out of you by simply talking to another man, I'd say you need to rethink making her yours."

On the elevator ride down Max figured it was definitely too late for that.

Chapter 11

Eating crow wasn't the easiest thing in the world for Max, but it wasn't the worst.

Noreen Lakefield answered the door, letting him into their suite. In the living room area, Paul Lakefield sat, a stern expression on his face.

Looking at them both, Max tried to relate them to the parents that Deena had described. Her mother looked gentle, but her eyes said she could be a force if she needed to be. Her father looked as disapproving and unyielding as Deena said he was. But Max had dealt with worse. This wasn't going to be easy. Then again, nothing in his life was.

"Mr. and Mrs. Lakefield, my name is Maxwell Donovan. I wanted to personally apologize for the scene I created tonight. It was a misunderstanding and I overreacted. I apologize," he said, standing before them both.

"Have a seat, Maxwell," Noreen said, taking her seat beside her husband.

"Why don't you tell us about you and our daughter?"

That was the last thing he wanted to talk about but Max accepted that he didn't have much choice. "We met over the summer in South Carolina. I was working on a project."

"And she was dillydallying like she always does," Paul Lakefield interrupted.

"No. Actually, she was working on her next novel. The one that will be released in February," Max heard himself saying.

"She told you about her books?" Noreen asked.

"Yes," Max answered. "She's very excited about her writing career."

Noreen nodded, a small smile forming. "And you two spent a lot of time together this summer?"

"Yes, we did. We, ah, grew very close over the summer. Then lost contact when we returned home. Seeing her again here was, ah, a shock."

"A shock," Noreen repeated. "You hadn't expected to ever see her again."

"No, ma'am, I hadn't."

"Why is that? You said you became close over the summer. Why would you want that to end?"

"It was a fling, Noreen. Deena's always doing something impulsive," Paul added.

Max clenched his teeth, trying to contain his annoyance with the way this man was talking about his daughter. "No, sir. It wasn't like that. We did become very close and it was actually my fault that we didn't see each other again. Deena, I think, was very committed to our relationship."

Noreen looked as if she knew something Max didn't. "But you weren't?"

"I wasn't sure what I wanted."

"And what you want now is to claim her as your woman so no other man can touch her. Is that it?" Paul asked.

This was a hard man to like, Max decided. But what he sensed undeniably was that Paul Lakefield loved his family, in his own way.

"I just want to apologize for the way I acted tonight. I was wrong. I shouldn't have put my hands on her that way and I shouldn't have made a scene."

"So what happens now between you and Deena?" Noreen asked.

"I honestly don't know."

"You can start by apologizing to her," Paul said gruffly. "She's in the suite on the other side of this floor."

That wasn't a part of his plan but Max wasn't going to sit there and argue that fact with her parents. Instead he stood, shaking Mr. Lakefield's hand. To his surprise Mrs. Lakefield pulled him in for a hug. The waters between the families working together weren't ruffled by his idiocy. That was enough to be grateful for.

And it should have been enough to get him on the elevator and out of that building to his own home where he would be safe to kick himself in private.

But it wasn't.

There was someone else he owed an apology, for more than just tonight. He might as well get all his apologizing out of the way at one time.

Her room was just down the hall from her parents.

Max hadn't planned to use the information, but now here he was.

He knocked and waited, knew she would look through the peephole before opening. So about a minute later he knocked again. She was angry, he couldn't blame her. She'd be thinking and rethinking whether or not to let him in. He could walk away now, say he'd given it a try. Just like he did when he'd stopped by her place in New York. But tonight, as he lay in his apartment alone, he'd think of what a coward he'd been. Again.

Lifting his arm, he prepared to knock once more. She pulled the door open instead.

She was still wearing the dress, the turquoise beaded material still clinging to every curve of her body. Her hair was down now, heavy twists resting at her shoulders. The smile he missed was gone, replaced by the tight line of her lips. The look in her eyes told him to go to hell. This distance between them made him feel like he was already there.

"What do you want? Haven't embarrassed me enough? You here for round two or should I say three?"

Max cleared his throat, the sight of her still made it go dry. "I'm here to apologize."

"So do it and go," she snapped.

"Deena—" He took a step toward her.

She put up both her hands, an act meant to ward him off. "Don't. I don't want to hear explanations or excuses. If you're apologizing, fine. I accept. Now go home."

She'd already stepped back, was preparing to close the door in his face. But Max wasn't leaving until they'd cleared the air. Even if they couldn't be together, they were going to end this in a civil manner. He owed it to both of them to make that happen. He put his body between the door.

"Move or I'll call the police."

"Ten minutes. That's all I'm asking for."

"No."

"Deena, let's not do this in the hallway where anybody could walk by and hear us."

"Let's not do this at all," she said tightly.

"You don't mean that. You've obviously got something to say to me. Let me in and you can get it off your chest. We'll have this out once and for all."

She stepped back and let him in. "Five minutes, then I'm calling the cops to throw your ass out."

Once inside the room Max heaved a sigh of relief, this was half the battle. He'd dealt with angry women before, but none he'd cared about. He didn't want to hurt Deena, never had. That's why he'd walked away before, aiming for a clean break. Obviously that was a bad idea.

Especially since he still wanted her. Desperately.

His jealous tirade had been fueled by his insatiable hunger for her. That hadn't subsided; no distance had taken that away. He'd thought about going to another woman, but substitutes weren't appealing. It was her he wanted. How he was going to deal with that from this moment on Max had no clue.

"First, let me say I'm sorry about not returning your calls when we returned from Hilton Head. It was rude of me and I wish I would have dealt with that situation better."

She'd sat at the bar, in one of the highboy chairs, her legs crossed, arms folded over her chest. "That's no news flash."

She was determined to make this hard for him. No way was he going to come in here and drop a sorry-ass apology then walk out. If that was the case he could go now. "I called you and I emailed you."

He pushed his hands into his pockets, stood with his legs slightly parted. The action pushed his jacket back so that the fit of his tuxedo shirt was on display. Did this man have a personal tailor? Every piece of clothing she'd ever seen him wear fit him with perfection. It made her sick. Or it aroused the hell out of her. She'd examine which one later.

"I know. I should have responded."

"Why didn't you?"

He paused, seeming to think about the question for a moment.

"If you're going to lie, don't bother. I'm so over the games right now."

He nodded as if he agreed. "I thought we needed a clean break."

And just like that it was. If it were remotely possible, Deena would swear her heart split in two the moment he spoke those words. "Fine," she said through clenched teeth.

"But tonight, when I saw you in Ben's arms. I don't know, I just lost it."

She'd slid off the chair, intending to walk away from him, but her legs weren't as strong as she thought. She turned her back to him instead, placing her hands on the edge of the bar to steady herself.

"Why?" she heard her own voice, small and vulnerable.

"I didn't like seeing another man's hands on you."

"But you don't want me."

"That's a lie. You said no more lies."

He was closer, she could hear his voice closer now. She closed her eyes, reaching deep inside for the strength to turn to him, to curse him and walk away. But it wasn't there. Damn it, it wasn't there.

"You look so damned beautiful in that dress. You were smiling at him, letting him touch you." He cleared his throat again. "I couldn't stand it."

The sound of his voice swirled around her, like a tortured soul. She cringed, wanted to break free, but couldn't. She was trapped. He hadn't put a hand on her but she knew she was trapped right there where she stood regardless.

"I don't understand. I don't know what you want from me, Max."

"Nothing," his words whispered over the bare skin of her back as he stepped closer. "And everything."

His lips brushed her shoulder. He couldn't not kiss her, not touch her. It was insane and he should have known better. But being in a room with Deena, this close, without touching her was not possible.

"Don't," she whispered. "Please don't do this to me."

"I can't stop."

He traced lines along her shoulder with his tongue, inhaling her scent, loving her taste. His hands went to the nape of her neck, found the clasp that held the dress up and unsnapped it. She gasped, the material slid down.

"Every time I close my eyes I see you. Every glorious inch of your naked body is emblazoned in my memory like a portrait of perfection."

His kisses trailed a heated line down her spine.

Deena sucked in a breath, her fingers gripping the side of the bar so hard her knuckles colored.

"I try to sleep at night but I feel you next to me. I feel your legs wrapping around mine, your arms embracing me."

The dress had hitched at her waist, she felt him push it down completely as tears burned the backs of her eyes. "Max," she moaned when his lips touched her butterfly tattoo.

"I need you, but I don't want to. I crave you, when I know I shouldn't. I can't stop. I just can't."

With those final words he pulled on the string of her thong until it snapped, falling to the floor to meet the dress.

It was wrong. He said he didn't want to want her. That should be enough to walk away. But it wasn't what he said that had her heart thumping wildly in her chest, her center aching for his touch. It was what he didn't say.

He loved her.

She turned. He was still in a kneeling position and he dropped a kiss over her clean-shaved mound.

"Maxwell," she said his name but it was more like giving him permission.

He looked up at her as he stood, grasping her waist and lifting her until she once again sat on the highboy chair.

Max spread her legs wide, tracing a finger down her dampened center as she moaned. Her fingers were on his belt, pulling it free of his pants. Then his zipper, ripping it down, reaching inside to pull out his engorged erection. In one swift motion she was pulled to the edge of the chair, he'd stepped closer. Their bodies met, melded, locked in a heated embrace.

His motions were fierce. Her legs wrapped around his waist tightly. They sighed and moaned, soared and climbed the pinnacle together. She heard him whisper her name, over and over and over again, like he was worshiping her.

She'd said his name, but in a different tone. Like she loved him.

Max carried her to the bathroom, setting her on her feet while he adjusted the spray and temperature of the water. When it was ready they stepped inside together.

He lathered a cloth and washed every inch of her body. Her eyes watched him, assessing his intentions, he knew. But Max had no idea what his intentions were. Originally, they'd been to come to this hotel and apologize to the people he'd embarrassed and wrongly accused. Then he'd planned to go home and sulk.

But here he was. And here she was. And it just seemed right.

When she took the same cloth and filled it with soap, touching his body similar to the way he'd done hers, he didn't know what to say. She was tender and thorough and his arousal grew once more. What was it about her that made him lose all control?

He took her, right there, one more time. With her in his arms, her back plastered against the tile of the shower, he entered her.

"Max," she moaned his name, wrapped her arms and legs around him tightly.

With every stroke he fell deeper, his heart filling

with her in ways he'd never anticipated. This wasn't planned and it wasn't right, yet he couldn't stop.

After bathing them once more, Max finally carried Deena to bed. He kissed her, trying to keep his doubts at bay. As he pulled away she reached out, touched his shoulders.

"I don't know what we're doing," he said, his words as tortured as his soul.

"Stay," she said simply, then moved aside, making a space for him in the bed beside her.

Max lay in that bed, Deena wrapped around him, her warmth a welcome pleasure in stark contrast to the lonely nights spent in his bed alone. He still didn't know what he was doing here, what this would mean for them in the morning. He had absolutely no more answers than he had this afternoon or six months ago.

And for right now, it didn't seem to matter. He had Deena.

Chapter 12

Through the heavy fog of sleep Deena struggled to wake. She heard noises that didn't quite go with the serene dream she was having. Turning over, she cracked one eye open and saw him.

His broad, muscled back was bare. He had on his pants and he was sitting on the side of the bed, his elbows resting on his knees, his head lowered.

"Max?"

"I've gotta go," he said without turning to face her.

Everything inside her was instantly awake, on alert. Deena shifted until she was sitting up in the middle of the bed, pulling the sheets up to cover her nakedness.

"Okay. My flight out isn't until later this evening." She took a deep breath and asked, "Will I see you before then?"

Max released a breath then stood, reaching over to

a chair that held the rest of his clothes. He slipped his arms into the shirt then turned to face her. "I don't think so."

She nodded. Refused to cry, absolutely would not give him that again. "So this is it? Again."

"Look, Deena, I know how it seems but it's really not like that."

Tucking the sheets under her arms she ran her hands through her hair. "Oh, you don't just like sleeping with me then leaving without a word? Is that what you want me to believe?"

His fingers paused momentarily over the buttons of the shirt. "I want you to believe that if I could do this any differently I would."

She nodded her head. "How about this? You're a coward, running away from feelings that scare you to death. You can handle the sex and the light conversations because then you don't have to give too much of yourself. You're a selfish, egotistical—"

"I can't give you what you want!" he yelled, interrupting her. "Is that what you want me to say, what you want me to admit to you? I cannot give you the kind of relationship you want or deserve."

Only the bottom half of his shirt was buttoned and he hadn't bothered to tuck it in. But he was grabbing his jacket and about to leave the room when her voice stopped him.

"How do you know what I want?" she asked quietly. "We've never even talked about relationships or futures. I think we've actually covered every other subject in the world but that."

"Don't do this, Deena. I'm begging you not to go

there. Why can't we just part friends? I don't want to hurt you."

"But you already have. And if you walk out that door right now I'll suffer just a little bit more than I have over the past six months." She sighed. "But I won't break, Max. I promise you I won't break or collapse into a million pieces. I can handle rejection—I just don't like not knowing why. So could you please just give me that."

The moment he turned to face her Max felt like he'd give her anything in the world. If he could reach up into the sky and pull down the sun for her, he would. So if all she needed was the truth, then he was going to give it to her.

"I'm sterile, Deena. I can never impregnate a woman. I'll never have kids of my own."

"What?" The question was a whisper, then she was shaking her head. "Wait a minute. You can't make babies. So you won't let yourself love or be loved. Is that what you're saying to me? Is that why you're leaving me?"

"You want a family, you said so yourself. You want the same happy endings you write about in your books. A husband and kids, your own family. I can't give you that."

"Can you love me?" she asked simply.

"I can't stop loving you."

Her lips curved in a shaky smile. "Then nothing else matters."

Pushing the sheets back, she climbed out of the bed, walking toward him. Wrapping her arms around his waist and burying her head against his chest she repeated, "Nothing else matters, Max. Because I can't stop loving you either."

"That's how you feel now but what about later? What happens when you're ready for more and I can't give it to you?"

She didn't hesitate. "Then we'll work it out. There are options, I'm sure. We can make this work, Max. I know we can."

She sounded so sure, so convinced. She thought she had all the answers. And Max, damn him, wanted to believe her.

He hadn't avoided her calls this time and had, in fact, sent her emails and text messages on his own. But as the days went by with her in New York and Max in Las Vegas, Deena began to feel like more than the physical distance was between them.

She was sitting in her favorite coffee shop and internet café on a Saturday afternoon, supposedly working. Her mind hadn't been on work since she'd returned home. It hadn't been on anything but Max, on what he'd told her. That's why instead of her screen being opened to a document, it was on the internet where she was searching sterility and alternative parenting. If this was what was standing between her and Max then she was determined to find a solution.

There were lots of things they could do. Depending on exactly what Max's condition was—that she didn't know because she'd been so busy trying to convince him that their love would be enough that she hadn't asked any details about it. Anyway, there were surgical options for some men that could fix the problem. And if not, they could try adopting. They could still have a happy future together, she just needed to come up with an answer.

Deena was so into her research that she hadn't heard anyone approach and sit down across from her.

"You still don't pay attention to your surroundings," Monica said as she reached over, using a palm to cover the screen of Deena's laptop.

"Oh," Deena said, momentarily startled. "Hey, Monica. What are you doing here?"

Today Monica wore jeans and a crisp white shirt. She probably had on some stiletto-heeled shoes, which she preferred, but Deena couldn't see under the table. Her hair was pulled back, but instead of being up in its usual bun, the curly ends hung loosely down her back. Her makeup and accessories were perfect, as usual. But she was here, in a coffee shop, with Deena. Not normal.

"I stopped by your place and you weren't there. I know this is your spot so I took a chance that you'd be here."

Deena nodded. This was her "spot" so to speak. "What'd you get? You hate coffee." She looked down at the steamy beverage sitting on the table in front of her sister.

"Hot chocolate," Monica answered.

"With whipped cream and chocolate shavings?"

Monica smiled. "Is there any other way?"

"Not for you. So what's going on? Why were you looking for me?"

"Just wanted to check on you."

Deena had turned her attention back to her laptop. "I'm fine."

"You missed brunch last week."

"I've got a deadline."

"That you're working on now?"

"Ah, yeah," Deena answered.

Monica reached out, grabbed the end of the laptop and turned it so that she could see the screen. "Sperm delivery problems. Ductal absence or blockage. Is this a part of your story?"

Deena frowned, taking her laptop back and closing it. "It's something I'm researching."

Monica arched a brow. "Why?"

"Because I'm interested."

"You're interested in sterility research?"

It sounded crazy but Deena wasn't going to be intimidated by Monica's interrogation. "Yes."

"Or are you interested in Maxwell Donovan, who at age twenty-one was in a brutal altercation on the campus of Tulane University?"

"What? How do you know about Max?" Deena hadn't told either of her sisters that Max was the man from Hilton Head. In fact, she hadn't even told her mother. She'd just said she'd met Max before. So how had Monica found out?

"Was he the man you met over the summer? The one who didn't call?"

"I asked my question first."

Monica lifted her cup to her lips, took a tentative sip. "First, everybody who can read and stands in line at a grocery store would have seen the picture and article they did on you and Donovan as you argued at the benefit in Las Vegas," she said matter-of-factly.

Deena hadn't known about any article. Had she really been that preoccupied?

"And a few weeks before you went to Las Vegas with Mom and Dad I came by your place to check on you and a man was ringing your buzzer. Naturally, I wanted to know who he was and what he wanted. He told me his name was Maxwell Donovan and that he was dropping by to see you, wanted me to let you know he'd stopped by."

"And you didn't tell me? Monica, how could you not tell me something like that? And why do you insist on checking up on me? I'm a grown woman—I can take care of myself."

"That's what you keep telling me," Monica said evenly. "But you know what, Deena? Actions speak a lot louder than words. What kind of woman goes to an island and has an affair with a man, then gives him her heart to trample all over when they return? Now, months later you're still hung up on this guy so much so that you're missing standing family engagements and letting your work slack."

"What kind of woman does that, you want to know, Monica? The kind of woman that isn't afraid to fall in love. The kind of woman that isn't intimidated by a man or too arrogant to admit she might need one."

"I don't need a man, Deena. I can do everything that needs to be done in my life on my own. You don't even know if this man wants you."

"If he came here to see me doesn't that tell you something?"

"He's not here now. Doesn't that tell *you* something?"

No, she wasn't going to let Monica win this battle. There was something between her and Max. "It tells me he has a life."

"One that doesn't include you. Now how long do you plan to let that go on?"

"You don't understand."

Monica sighed. "Unfortunately, Deena, I do. You're hopelessly in love with this man. And from what I could see when I met him, he has some feelings for you. My question is, what are you going to do about it?"

Deena didn't know how to take her sister's words. First of all, they didn't really sound like something Monica would say. Then again, ever since her own college years, Monica hadn't been the same. Deena and Karena figured something had happened while Monica was away at school but their big sister had never spoken of it so they'd just let it drop. But since graduating and coming back to New York Monica had been an ice queen. Nothing touched her, not men, not work issues, nothing. And the only people she allowed even partially into her life was her immediate family.

"He told me that he's sterile and that because he can never offer me the family that I eventually want, we shouldn't be together."

Monica nodded. "And so you, what, are trying to find a way to fix his sterility problem? Do you think that will make everything better?"

"Of course it will. If Max can be fixed then we can be together without all this stress."

"Listen to yourself, Deena. 'If Max can be fixed.' He's not a dog. He's a man. And you can't just go around 'fixing' a man. It never works." Monica was sounding like she'd had this sort of experience.

"I'm not trying to change him. Just make him—"

"Make him what?" Monica interrupted. "Better? By whose standards?"

Deena shook her head. "You're mixing up my words. I don't even know why I'm talking to you about this."

Monica sipped from her cup again. "Because I'm

your sister and despite how stubborn you are, you need help. Mom and Karena want to dance around these issues with you, they always have. But it's time you had a hard talking-to."

"But I don't need it from you," Deena said, standing to leave.

"Sit down. Don't make a scene," Monica said, her voice a fraction lower than it had been.

"Why? Because you don't want the precious Lakefield name blasted in the papers for having an argument in a public place?"

"No, even though you've had enough negative press lately. But because now that Mom is hooked up with the Donovans, there's more than just our name on the line. See, Deena, you've always thought everything revolved around you. Deena wants to play guitar. Deena wants to take ballet. Deena wants to go to Europe. Deena wants…Deena needs…Deena takes. It's time for Deena to grow up."

Deena wanted to reach across the table and slap her sister's perfect face. But what would that prove? That Monica, the perfect, was right? With a heavy sigh Deena sat down.

"I don't want to fight with you, Monica."

"I didn't come here to fight."

"Then why did you come?"

"To show my sister that despite what she thinks I'm here for her. If it's to be a shoulder to lean on because some man has broken your heart, then that's what I'll be. If it's to give you a kick in the butt when you're being a spoiled, selfish brat, then that's what I'll do too. Because I love you, Deena, and I only want what's best for you."

Deena didn't smile, but her sister's words warmed her heart. "What would be really good for me right now is to have some of that hot chocolate."

Both sisters grinned as Monica pushed her cup across the table to sit in front of Deena. When her younger sister took a swallow, Monica sat back in her chair.

"Now, what are we going to do about this man of yours?"

Chapter 13

It was late that evening when Deena tried to call Max. She'd wanted to hear his voice and to get his thoughts on the research she'd done this afternoon. Not that she wasn't taking Monica's observations about trying to change him into consideration, she just wanted to let him know that she was there for him and that she was thinking of him. But he didn't answer.

So instead, she sent him an email noting a couple of the websites she'd visited for information. She was just going through emails from her publicist about book signing dates and locations when there was a knock at her door. It was after eleven and she was more than a little curious about who'd be at her door this time of night.

Slipping on her robe, she made her way to the door and was surprised to see Kevin standing on the other side. Well, not exactly surprised. She'd known he would show up sooner or later, but was really banking on later.

"Hi," he said with a friendly smile.

"Hi, Kevin." She tried to sound just as friendly.

When Deena had returned from Las Vegas, after being with Max again, she'd known without a doubt that there was nothing between her and Kevin. She'd called him upon her return and tried to do the breakup thing over the phone. Kevin wasn't very receptive to what she was saying, but he was also in the middle of a major deal with one of his clients so he couldn't really devote his full attention to the end of their relationship. She'd sort of let the situation die as he hadn't called her and she hadn't thought of him in the past few days. She actually hoped he'd just keep it moving. But something told her Kevin wasn't that type of guy.

"I've been trying to get a hold of you all day. Can I come in?"

It was late and she was already dressed for bed, but Deena stepped to the side and let him in. She was certain this wasn't going to be a conversation she wanted her neighbors to hear.

When they were in her living room, Kevin took a seat first. "So how have you been?" he asked, rubbing his hands up and down his jean-clad thighs.

Since he'd taken the couch Deena sat in the single chair across from him. "I've been good. Working. What brings you by this time of night?" she asked, not really wanting this to be prolonged.

He shrugged. "I just thought we'd talk. We really didn't have a chance to do that when you came back."

"I called you as soon as I returned," she said.

He nodded. "I know. I guess I didn't have the opportunity to say the things I wanted to say."

"Okay." That was fair. If she'd had her say, he should definitely be able to have his.

"I thought we were heading in a good direction," he began. She opened her mouth to speak. He gave her an expectant stare and she stopped.

"When I first received your online query for representation I thought your name sounded familiar, so I did a little background checking on you."

Deena supposed that could be construed as normal. One would definitely want to know who they were considering working with. However, she didn't think that was general protocol for all literary agents. Anyway, she didn't feel like examining the issue.

"The first time I saw your picture I thought you were absolutely beautiful. Your eyes were so full of life, your smile so sure of happiness. I wanted to meet you. I don't usually meet up with potential clients. A phone call is the norm."

His hands still moved over his thighs but his eyes remained fixed on hers. For a minute it seemed like a nervous action, but Kevin had never been nervous around her before.

"You were even more spectacular in person. I wanted…" He hesitated. "I wanted so much more than to represent you."

He stopped talking and just stared at her. It was beginning to feel creepy, having him here in the middle of the night, talking to her about his thoughts after simply receiving an email from her. She remembered their lunch and thought it was a nice professional meeting. She hadn't thought about him romantically at all. His call to her weeks later was a surprise and, if truth be told, the only reason she agreed to go out with him was because she was feeling so crappy about Max. Not because of any type of attraction to him personally. Maybe that was wrong, but in the beginning she'd hoped that she could develop some sort of connection with Kevin to get her over Max. Yeah, it was wrong; it was rebound and she shouldn't have done it.

"Listen, Kevin. I'm sorry if I gave you the wrong impression. I guess it does seem like I led you on. But I was just coming out of a relationship when we started seeing each other. I guess I wasn't really over him so it was unfair to start seeing you. I hope you can accept my apology."

Kevin laughed, his usual dark somber eyes holding an unfamiliar gleam. He'd worn a black shirt to go with his dark jeans and soft-bottom black shoes. He normally didn't dress this casual. Then again, she didn't normally see him at this time of night.

"You want to apologize?" he asked through laughter that sounded more creepy than the mere fact that he was here in the first place. "Is that what you're saying?"

Deena nodded, taking a deep swallow. "Yes, that's what I'm saying."

From the bedroom Deena could hear her cell phone ringing. She stood up to go and answer it, but Kevin stood too. Grabbing her by the arm, his smile turned to a grimace, that gleam in his eyes pinning her with an icy glare.

"If you're going to apologize for anything it's for being a conniving little slut!"

"What…get off of me!" she yelled into his face. "Get out of my house!"

"You're a tease and a slut. Why don't you admit to that, Deena! Why don't you tell the truth for once?"

He'd grabbed her other arm then and began shaking her as he yelled. "You played me. I'll admit it. Did you get a good laugh about that? You and your stuck-up sisters, did you all laugh behind my back at what a fool you were making of me?"

Her teeth clanked together he was shaking her so hard. The sound echoed in her head. His grip on her arms was so tight she thought she could feel the pinch of his nails. This could not be happening. Creepy was now turning into possibly deadly. This kind of crazy stalker mess happened in made-for-TV movies, not in real life. Not in her life.

"Listen, Kevin." She tried for calm. Maybe she could reason with him. "I do apologize for whatever wrong you think I may have done to you. Like I said, that wasn't my intention."

"Intention? I know exactly what your intention was. You wanted to string me along, make your rich boyfriend jealous. Well, I don't give a damn about him, or you for that matter!"

With those words Kevin tossed her down on the floor. She made the connection with a sickening thump that knocked the wind out of her. Coughing and trying to breathe normally, Deena attempted to crawl away from him. Her house phone was ringing now. She wanted desperately to get to it. Not necessarily to answer but at least to knock it off the base so someone could hear what was going on and send for help.

But Kevin grabbed her by the legs, dragging her across the floor, toward the bedroom.

"I'm going to get what I want, what you teased me

with all these weeks. Rich-boy Donovan got it so why shouldn't I? That's right, I saw your picture all over the tabloids with him dragging you around. You liked it when he got rough with you and you gave it up to him."

Her robe had come open and the carpet was burning against the bare skin of her stomach and legs as he pulled her along. Trying to break free of his grasp put her at an awkward angle so that she thought her shoulders would rip right from the sockets. She kicked her feet, yelling for him to stop. She couldn't let him get her into the bedroom. The mere thought of what he planned to do had fear rising in her like a heated flame. When they were at the door Deena spread her legs, blocking the entrance.

"Yeah, you're used to opening those legs. But not just yet. Not yet," he growled as he bent over, punching her knees so that they'd bend with the pain. He yanked her through the doorway then let her drop in the center of the floor.

Her phone was ringing again. But now the sound seemed distant.

Kevin was standing over her, his hands undoing the button and zipper of his pants. Deena saw red, fury blinding everything else. He was not going to rape her, not as long as she had breath in her. Lifting her legs she kicked directly at his groin, satisfied with the rugged groan that tore from him with her efforts. Rolling over she pushed up off the floor, searching the room frantically for something, anything. He was coming for her again, this time lunging and grabbing a fistful of her clothes. The front of her nightgown tore and Deena screamed.

He pushed her against the wall before she could

find something to hit him with. She swung wildly, not knowing where exactly she was hitting him, but feeling her fists making connections. Kevin didn't seem at all bothered by her hits, he was only focused on one thing. His hands still fumbled with his pants, his legs pushing hers open.

Deena screamed like she'd seen in horror movies and prayed she'd never have to do in her lifetime. Her throat burned, tears streaming down her face.

Then everything went black.

She saw nothing. Felt nothing.

Chapter 14

"What are you doing, Maxwell?" Alma Donovan asked the moment she stepped into Max's apartment.

"I don't know what you mean," he answered, closing the door behind her and following her into the living room.

"Ben told me all about you and Deena Lakefield. He also told me why you think behaving like a jackass is the right thing to do."

Max frowned. Ben was a grown man and still couldn't hold a bucket of water. Whatever he knew he told, just like when they were kids.

"It's not necessary. I have it under control," Max started to say.

"Take a seat and humor me," Alma said in her efficient manner.

There was no getting around this, Max knew. So he

simply took a seat and a deep breath. "Like I told you before, we met in South Carolina. We liked each other and decided to spend the summer together. When my work was done I came home. She went back to her home in New York. That's it."

"That's not it. Is this woman in love with you?"

"She says she is."

"And are you in love with her?"

"It doesn't matter, Mom. Love isn't always enough. Especially not in my situation."

Alma folded her hands in her lap. "And what exactly is your situation, Maxwell?"

Whenever she called him by his full name Max knew the conversation wasn't going to go the way he wanted. "I'm not like other men. I can't offer her the same things they can."

"Did she ask you for something specific?"

"No."

"Then how do you know if what you have isn't enough for her?"

"Mom," he sighed.

"Don't 'Mom' me. I thought I'd raised a smarter child than this. I can't believe you're sitting here believing this nonsense. If this woman loves you and you love her, then there's no problem."

"You know what the problem is."

"I know you now have an unfortunate diagnosis because you tried to do the right thing. But I also know that only the grace of God brought you out of that hospital alive. With as much blood as you lost, you could have died. At that point I didn't care if we had to roll you out of that hospital in a wheelchair, as long as you were breathing." Her voice hitched on the last words.

Great, now he'd made his mother cry.

"Mom, I know. I didn't mean to bring up bad memories."

"No. You don't mean to live the full life that you were given. And that's like blasphemy, Maxwell."

"I don't think—" he started to say.

"It is. You listen to me. You are a good man. You're handsome and you're intelligent—at least most of the time. You've got a good business going, your own place. You have a lot to offer a woman. And a good woman would be able to see this. I get the impression that Deena Lakefield's a good woman."

"She is," he admitted.

"Then she doesn't deserve this. No woman deserves to be pushed aside because you can't get your emotional issues in check. Now I want you to think long and hard about that, Maxwell. Think about somebody else besides yourself, you might be surprised what you come up with."

But Max wasn't surprised. As he read the latest email from Deena two hours after his mother's impromptu visit, he knew what he had to do.

He hit Send and sighed. This was it. He promised himself and her, there would be no more.

He'd read her latest email three times, a fireball of guilt in his gut growing each time. Six months ago he'd met Deena Lakefield at a summer resort. In that time he'd slept with her, left her, embarrassed her in front of hundreds of people including her parents, slept with her again, dumped his emotional and physical baggage on her and now this. Now, she was trying to help him, to "fix" him. How much more did he expect her to carry?

It was wrong. She should have happiness, a man that loved her completely and could give her any and everything she needed and wanted. She didn't need him.

No matter how much he loved her, and he did. It wasn't so hard to admit now that he was in love with the vivacious and compassionate romance author. And he wanted her more than he wanted his next breath.

But it wasn't enough. She deserved more.

And he'd told her just that in what he swore would be his last email message to her. He wouldn't contact her anymore, and he had asked her not to contact him. What they had was done and it was for the best. She needed to move on.

It was almost nine-thirty on a Friday night and he was in his apartment, alone. He was doing the family name a disservice when it came to women. His own philandering reputation was dismal in comparison to the other Donovan men, but Max didn't mind. In fact, he doubted philandering had any more appeal to him now than it had before he'd met Deena. He'd avoided it for just this reason.

Switching off his computer he went to the living room and turned on his CD player. Five discs were already inserted, he listened to them so frequently. Moving to the minibar, he fixed himself a glass of rum, then took his glass and the bottle over to the couch where he plopped down.

The way he'd arranged his furniture he could sit right here and look out his patio doors. His apartment was on the fourteenth floor so he had an unfettered view of the brim of the city lights, a stretch of desert land and the caps of the mountains.

Lifting his glass to his lips the smooth sound of the first song on Miles Davis's *Kind of Blue* CD began to play.

It was fitting, Max thought as he took another sip and another. The pain he was feeling only Miles could decipher, only the irresistible sound of the trumpet could portray.

"Hello?" His mouth felt full of cotton or something dry and frankly distasteful. Max coughed, cleared his throat and tried again. "Hello?"

The phone had been ringing for what seemed like ages. At first he'd thought it was a dream or a hallucination, considering he'd finished that bottle of rum two CDs ago. He was laying facedown on the couch, the glass and bottle on the floor, the music still playing in the background as he'd set it to repeat.

"I said, this is Monica Lakefield."

"Who?"

"Monica Lakefield. Look, I have to tell you something about Deena."

Hearing her name was like a splash of cold water to his face. Max sat up in the chair. Actually, he slid off the edge of the chair as he was trying to sit up, but he held the phone steady to his ear. "Deena? Who is this again?"

The sound of irritation was clear in the female voice as she spoke again. "This is Monica Lakefield. I'm Deena's sister. Something's happened," she said.

"What? What happened?" Max asked, holding his breath, not really sure he was ready for the answer.

"Deena was attacked tonight. In her apartment. She's at the hospital. I don't know if you care or…whatever. I just thought you should know," she said in a clipped tone.

"Where? What hospital?" was all Max said and once he'd received the answer he hung up.

His next call was to Linc. "I need the private jet," he said the moment his cousin answered the phone.

"Now? It's almost eleven o'clock. Where are you going?"

Already up and walking toward his bedroom so he could change, Max said, "I don't have time for a Q&A, Linc. I need the jet fueled and ready to go in twenty minutes. I'll explain later."

"Sure, but you mind telling me where you're taking the jet? I mean, that's a small fact the pilot might want to know."

"I'm going to New York," was his answer.

Adam and Ben were waiting for him when he boarded the jet with his overnight bag. Max wasn't really surprised but the last thing he felt like doing right now was talking about what was going on.

The truth of the matter was he didn't know. All he knew for certain was that he'd ended things for good between him and Deena via email. Then he'd resigned himself to drink away his misery. But the phone rang and it was her sister; Deena was hurt. And nothing else, not his sterility, not what was best for who or what decisions he had to make, mattered.

His only thought now was getting to Deena, ensuring she was all right.

The plane took off and there was silence in the open

cabin. Max was belted in his seat. Across from him sat Adam and in the comfortable matching leather seat behind him was Ben. Nobody said a word for the first hour of the flight.

"What happened?" Adam asked finally.

Max had been staring out the window, looking at the pitch-black sky, feeling exactly the same way inside. "I don't know."

"Someone had to call and tell you something. What's going on, Max?"

"She's hurt, that's all I know. Her sister called and said she'd been attacked. I don't know anything else."

Behind him Ben's cell phone rang. He heard his brother speaking in a low murmur then a few minutes later disconnected.

"Trent was able to get in touch with Sam. You know Sam's brother Cole is a detective. Well, he heard on the police radar about an attack and possible rape at an apartment building in Manhattan. Cole lives and works in Greenwich but I guess his radar picks up everything in the vicinity. I don't know. But at the same time, Sam was calling Cole because Karena had received a call from her sister. It was Deena, Max."

He didn't move. Not a muscle in his entire body could move as he heard the words. His gaze didn't waver from the dark sky, but memories of a similar night assaulted him. And rage held him perfectly still as tears glazed his eyes.

"Ben, call Sam and make sure the best doctors are there with her," Adam instructed. "She's going to be okay, Max. We'll be there soon."

But soon wasn't fast enough.

Chapter 15

The hospital room was dark and cold and sterile. And even though he walked in, let the door close quietly behind him and kept moving until he was only a couple inches away from her, Max still felt like he was on the other side of the world.

Nothing he'd done in his life, nothing he'd ever felt or ever had to deal with compared to this very moment.

The room was silent except for the low beeping of a box-type machine, hitched on a pole on the other side of the bed. Numbers flashed on the machine then went bold and the beeping stopped. His gaze flew to her face, down to her chest where the rhythmic rise and fall assured him that she was breathing just fine.

Contusions and a minor concussion is what the doctor had told them when they arrived. In the waiting room Mr. and Mrs. Lakefield sat. Max had gone to them first, almost afraid of the response he would get.

Paul Lakefield stood, giving Max a stern look. "What are you doing here?"

Max answered, "I heard she was hurt. How's she doing? Can you tell me what happened?"

The look on Paul's face said he was more than hesitant, but then Noreen stood, a hand touching Paul's arm slightly. She smiled up at Max, a watery smile as she dabbed at her tear-filled eyes once more. "Some maniac tried to…he tried to…" Noreen couldn't get the rest out before her head was buried in Paul's chest, sobs shaking her entire body.

"He tried but he didn't succeed. The doctor's already checked. But she hit her head on something at some point and she's been unconscious for hours."

Max knew that voice. Turning around to face it he wasn't really surprised to see the woman who'd been in Deena's apartment building that day. He'd known she knew Deena personally, and now it was confirmed.

"Monica?" he asked.

She nodded. "I'd been trying to call her all night and she just wasn't answering. So I went over to her apartment and there he was."

"There 'who' was? And how did he get in?" Max asked, his body trembling with anger. "Where is he now?"

"Calm down, Max. This isn't going to help. Why don't you just go see Deena and we'll get more specifics about what happened," Adam said standing close to Max's side.

"You'll feel better knowing that he's in custody," Sam offered, leaving the seat he was sitting in, holding

Karena's hand. "Cole is actually at the precinct now making sure he stays there for a good while."

"What was he? Her boyfriend?" The words stuck in Max's throat, his head throbbing at the sound.

"I thought that was you," Monica said snidely. Her face was blank but for the redness of her eyes and while she stood tall, giving the impression of strength, as she folded her arms over her chest, Max could see her hands shaking.

"Just go to her," Adam said.

Sam nodded his agreement.

And so he'd left them all standing there. He'd walked down what seemed like the longest hall in history to get to her room. And now stood here staring down at her as if he didn't know her at all.

Max remembered the hospital all too well. He remembered when it was him laying in the bed, beneath the stiff white sheets, IVs in his arm, oxygen going through his nose. Closing his eyes, he inhaled and tried to push back the crisp antiseptic smell.

Memories assailed him and he clenched his teeth, trying to bear all that had happened, his feelings for this woman, his past and what would become of his future.

"Max," she spoke in a raspy voice that jolted him out of his reverie.

Taking a step closer he touched her hand. "I'm here, baby. Don't try to move."

She was shifting like she wanted to sit up. "You're here," she said then touched a hand to her head where there was a white bandage. "Why? How?"

"Shh. You shouldn't get too excited."

"But what happened?" she asked.

Max knew, from her expression, she had answered

her own question. Deena now had horrific memories of her own. And Max hated that.

"It's okay, baby. Everything's going to be okay."

Tears filled her eyes as she pulled the sheets up to her neck. "He…he touched me and he said…said he wanted to…"

Max was shaking his head, using his free hand to wipe the tears from her face. "He didn't. He didn't do that."

Relief had her shoulders sagging into the bed. "I didn't know he would do that. I didn't know."

"I know you didn't. You don't have to explain."

"I told him we couldn't be together because I was in love with you. He was very angry with me."

So she'd rejected this man and he'd decided to make her pay for that rejection. Ass! What he wouldn't give for just five minutes alone with the jerk. He planned to see if Cole Desdune could work that out for him.

"It's all over now. Just try to rest."

"You came. How did you know to come?"

"Monica called me."

"Monica? Are you sure it wasn't Karena?"

Max chuckled, understanding her questioning. Monica didn't seem like she gave a damn about him or anybody else but herself. But she had in fact called him and given him the information. For that, no matter what else the woman did or didn't do, he would be forever grateful.

"She called and you came." She tried to smile but it must have been painful because she winced.

He'd noticed the purplish bruise on her right cheekbone and reached out a hand to lightly touch it. "Of course I came. The thought of something happening to you…" His words broke off. "I'm just glad you're safe now." Leaning over, he kissed her cheek then softly on her lips.

"I'm glad you're here. I love you," she whispered.

He could have ignored the words, pushed them out of his mind, but Max was through fighting. Tonight could have ended much differently than it had. This lunatic could have raped or, worse, killed her. He could have lost her forever. No amount of painful memories could compete with the fear he'd felt when he heard she was attacked. During his plane ride out here he'd had the time to think about his decision to walk away from her and realized it could be construed as being selfish. Although that wasn't the way he'd meant it, he could see how thinking about his own shortcomings and not considering Deena's feelings for him was unfair.

"I love you, too, Deena," he whispered right back, kissing her lips once more. "I love you so very much."

From his suite at the hotel Max could see the continuous stream of people enjoying Central Park on a Saturday afternoon. Adam and Ben had made the reservation and checked in while he'd stayed at the hospital with Deena. Her parents were with her when he left her a little over an hour ago. He was going back as soon as he finished here.

"You should eat something," Ben was saying when the room service guy had left. There were four trays of food in the living room area. But Max wasn't hungry.

"Not right now."

"You need to keep up your strength," Ben was saying as clearly as was possible around half the croissant he'd stuck in his mouth.

Max frowned. "Okay, Mom, I'll eat a little later."

"Hardheaded." Ben shrugged and kept chewing.

In one of the chairs near the window was Detective Cole Desdune. Across from him was Sam and another gentleman Max hadn't had the pleasure of meeting yet. He'd jumped in the shower as soon as he arrived. When he came out, just about fifteen minutes ago, all the guests were here.

Sam stood, extended a hand to Max. "How are you holding up?"

Max nodded and shook his hand. "I'm okay. Then again, I'm not the one that was attacked."

Cole flipped open a file he'd been holding on his lap. "Kevin Langley, thirty years old, business address in central Manhattan. Home address in Brooklyn. A member of AAR—Association for Author's Representatives—since two thousand. Fourteen clients, including best-selling Corigan Sellers. No wife, no kids, no family."

"No brain," Max grumbled. "He messed with the wrong woman."

"True. He also has no criminal record so they were seriously considering bail," Cole added.

"Are you kidding me?"

"Calm down. The Lakefields are pretty reputable here in the city. Bail's set at two point five million. Langley's got twenty-five grand in his operating account, forty-five hundred in his personal checking and seventeen hundred in his savings. He's not making bail anytime soon."

"The good thing is that Deena's okay. Alex's cousin has privileges at the hospital, he's going to examine her today," Sam said.

Max was dragging a hand down his face when he looked over at the stranger dressed in a suit sitting on the couch.

"Alex Bennett," the man said, standing to extend a hand to Max. "Sam's my brother-in-law."

Shaking his hand, Max remembered. "Your brother's married to his sister, right? My mom's also working with your relatives in Brazil with the children. I've heard a lot about your family. Thanks for your help."

"Don't mention it. We're all family here. When I heard about what happened to Deena I was pretty pissed myself. I despise men who can't take no for an answer."

"You and me both," Max said, finally taking a seat. "So your cousin, he's good?"

"He's the best. A world-renowned neurologist. I told him about her concussion. He was headed there about an hour ago so she's in good hands. And from what I can tell Cole's working along with the NYPD to keep the disgruntled ex in jail until trial time."

"Good." Max took the cup of coffee Adam handed him, sipped, then coughed. "Man, what are you trying to do to me? This tastes like—"

"It tastes like coffee, Max. You always put too much sugar in it. Just drink and keep quiet. We're just here to make sure you don't go down to the police station and handle Langley yourself."

They knew him too well. From the moment he'd heard what happened, seen Deena lying in the hospital bed, he'd seen red. Rage was engulfing him, his fingers itching to hit somebody, namely Kevin Langley. Just like when he was back in college.

"I'm not twenty-one anymore," he said through clenched teeth.

"True," Ben said. "But you've never been in love before either. So Adam and I thought the best thing we could do was to assure you that, one, Langley was safely tucked in jail and, two, Deena's going to be well taken care of."

"So I wouldn't find the man and beat the spit out of him?" Max asked, looking at all the concerned eyes around the room. He doubted that Max and Ben had told Cole, Sam and Alex about everything that had happened that night back in college, but they'd obviously told them about his notorious temper.

"Exactly," Cole said. "I'm out of my jurisdiction here, but Deena's family so they're lending me some courtesy. I'm not about to let him walk on this."

"I appreciate that. Really, I appreciate all your help. If Monica hadn't called me I don't know what I would have done hearing this later."

"So you've met the infamous Monica Lakefield," Sam said with a grin. "Tell me, what'd you think?"

Across from him Alex groaned. "If he's wise he didn't think about her for one minute. Ice-cold—"

"Hey. Hey. Watch it man, she's about to be my sister-in-law," Sam interjected.

"She was something at the hospital last night," Adam said. "I tell you what, I wouldn't want to be on the opposite side of a business deal with her. She's got a cutthroat air to her that I wouldn't want to go against."

"That's not all she's got," Ben said. "Did you see those legs?"

"Dangerous," Alex said. "The whole package has a big *D* written all over it."

Sam laughed. "She's really not that bad once you get to know her."

"You have to say that since you're marrying her sister," Alex said. "And you, since you're in love with her other sister, I guess you'll have to defend her, too."

He was talking to Max. It was the second time one of them had mentioned him being in love with Deena. At this point, Max wasn't even going to deny it.

"I owe her one for calling me and getting me out here, so I guess I will have to defend her. I think she really loves her family. As for the rest of us, she could probably chew us up and spit us out as her mid-morning snack. We'd do best not to get in her way."

The men laughed. All except Alex.

But Max was too preoccupied to really notice. He wanted to get back to the hospital. To get back to Deena.

Later that night, about an hour before visiting hours were over, Max and Deena were in her hospital room alone. She'd just finished eating her dinner and the television was playing some drama with Jada Pinkett Smith. They weren't watching but talking quietly as he sat on the side of her bed, holding her hand.

"You've got to promise me you won't let any more men into your apartment in the middle of the night," he said lightly even though the thought of her seeing this other man still had him in knots.

"Kevin was a mistake. I know that now. I make a lot of those," she said, staring out the window.

He hadn't meant to make her sad, just to tell her to be careful. He rubbed her hand. "We all make mistakes," he said. "It's the lesson we learn from them that counts. Just be careful from now on. You almost gave me a heart attack."

She smiled up at him. "Sorry. But I'm really glad you're here."

There was her smile again. It wasn't even the slightest bit marred by the bruises or the haphazard state of her hair. To Max, she was even more beautiful than she'd ever been. And he loved her more than he could ever say.

"I don't want to be anyplace else," he told her before leaning over and kissing her cheek.

"Come on, don't I deserve more than that?" she asked teasingly.

Now it was his turn to smile. "I guess we both do."

He kissed her again, this time on the lips. A light touch at first, then applying more pressure, slipping his tongue between her lips to claim hers. If it were possible considering the circumstances, this had to be one of the hottest kisses Max had ever experienced.

Deena's free hand came up to cup the back of his neck, pulling him down closer. She slanted her head and orchestrated one sensuous dance with her tongue over his. His body tightened with arousal even as he braced himself not to let his weight rest on top of her.

He suckled her tongue. She bit his lip. He groaned and she whimpered.

"We cannot have sex in this hospital bed," he mumbled against her lips.

"It is a bed." She sighed, kissing his chin.

"You have a concussion and bumps and bruises."

"Mmm-hmm. And I'll bet you're as hard as—"

"Attention all visitors. Visiting hours are over in five minutes," a shrill voice from the intercom echoed.

Max groaned again.

"Saved by the hospital administration," Deena said with a light laugh.

"I love you," Max said suddenly. Just like that he'd had to tell her, to say it again. He really loved this woman.

"Good. Because I love you, too."

Chapter 16

"I'm fine, Mama," Deena said as Karena adjusted another pillow behind her back two days later.

"I just don't think you should be working. You've just been through a terrible ordeal," Noreen was saying.

"I know and I'm not technically working," Deena argued.

Karena was the first to give in to her incessant requests for her laptop. Deena hated for her emails to build up and after two days of not checking them, she was sure her inbox was a nightmare.

The doctor, a top neurologist, who also happened to be the cousin of Alex Bennett, had insisted she stay in the hospital two days for observation. Deena felt like she was about to lose her mind. She wanted to go home. No, she wanted to get out of this hospital and go on that dinner and dancing date that Max had promised her.

Yes, Max was still in New York, to Deena's great delight. He'd stayed hours at the hospital with her every day. Taking Monica's advice, they hadn't talked at all about his condition or his reservations about their relationship. She hadn't wanted to destroy the time they had together. Besides, none of that mattered to her anymore. All she knew was that she was in love with Max, a loyal son, a generous lover and a great man.

"She won't be on long, Mom. Dr. Bennett says he's discharging her at noon," Karena said.

"Does Max know that?" Noreen asked.

Monica sighed. "Of course he does. He's been interrogating that doctor every day, ten times a day since she's been in here. I doubt there's anything he doesn't know about Deena's condition at the moment."

"I like him," Karena said. "Sam says he and Adam have built a really good business."

"I know his mother's very proud of him," Noreen offered. "I talked to her last night and she couldn't stop talking about the place he fixed up for her in Hilton Head. Said they're all heading there in a couple of months for the grand reopening."

"Yeah, Max said it's scheduled for Fourth of July. I think it's going to be great," Deena said, pushing the button and waiting for her computer to boot up.

"So when are you leaving?" Monica asked from her chair near the bottom of Deena's hospital bed.

"Leaving?"

"Aren't you going back to Las Vegas with your man?"

Nobody spoke. Noreen gave Deena a worried expression. Karena fidgeted with the blankets on Deena's bed. Monica's legs were crossed, her nails drumming over her knee. As for Deena, she looked away from all of them, focusing on her computer and typing in the log-in to her email. "Nobody's said anything about me moving to Vegas."

"Hmph," Monica said.

"It's too soon to think about a big move like that. You've been through a terrible time—you need time for yourself to get over what happened."

"That," Deena said with positivity, "I am so over. Just like I told Cole Desdune and the New York police, I don't need any counseling. I know it wasn't my fault that Kevin was a crazy stalker. There was nothing I could have done differently. He'd already fixated on me before I even went out with him."

At least that was how she felt on the outside. On the inside, she admitted to herself that the entire episode still had her a little shaky. But she'd never been one to give in to emotional breakdowns or fears that were big enough to overtake her. She'd misjudged Kevin Langley. It was unfortunate, yet she was blessed to be alive and to have not been assaulted sexually. For that she was grateful and would not hinder that gratitude with regrets.

"I know, sweetheart, but still it's trying to be brutally attacked and almost violated," Noreen insisted.

"It is, but I'm just not going to dwell on that. I have my family close by and that's all that matters."

"That and having your man close by, too," Monica added. "How long is he staying since you haven't talked about your move to Vegas?"

"Okay, Monica that's enough. She said they hadn't· talked about that," Karena said.

"Hadn't talked about it doesn't mean she isn't

thinking it. You are thinking about moving all the way to Vegas with him aren't you?"

It was an accusatory tone, which wasn't new coming from Monica. But Deena really wasn't in the mood for it. Besides, what she and Max decided or when they decided it was her business. "I'm not talking about this with you."

"Fine." Monica uncrossed her legs and stood. "I have work to do back at the gallery. Karena, I'm sure you do, too."

"We'll just stay until Max arrives," Noreen said.

Monica shook her head. "I'm leaving." She moved past her mother to give Deena a brisk kiss on the forehead. "Be good. I'll come by your apartment tonight to check on you."

And she would, Deena thought. Monica enjoyed checking on her, the little sister. But she couldn't be mad at her for it, refused to be at this point. Because if Monica hadn't stopped by to check on her Lord only knows what Kevin would have done to her unconscious body. When Monica arrived she'd had to hit him in the head with the DVD player to get him off of Deena. She hit him one too many times and knocked him out cold, then she'd called the police. So, from that moment on Deena vowed to be forever grateful for her big sister's interference in her life, at least marginally.

"See you later," Deena said, not bothering to look up because she could already hear the heels of Monica's shoes clicking across the floor.

"Sam and I will stop by, too. Is there anything you want me to bring you?"

"A hot dog with mustard and relish and a grape soda," she said automatically.

Karena chuckled as she mimicked Monica's motions of kissing her sister's forehead.

"You don't have to stay, Mom. I know you have a lot to do with the foundation stationed here and up and running," Deena told Noreen.

"Since when has anything in my life ever been as important as my girls?"

"Never," Deena answered. "But there's always a first for everything. Besides, I know it's not that business is more important. But you've all been here around-the-clock with me. I'm fine. Kevin's in jail and Dr. Bennett's taking good care of me. Now, go."

Noreen hesitated a moment. "You don't have to tell me when I'm not wanted," she said. "You be good until I see you tonight."

Unlike the other two, Noreen kissed her daughter's cheek before leaving. "Love you."

"Love you, too," Deena said then sighed with relief when she was finally alone.

But that relief was short-lived as she opened an email…from Max.

The room was empty when Max walked in and his heart did a stop and stammer. He looked around, saw her bag and purse on the chair but didn't see Deena. Dr. Bennett had just signed her discharge papers, but the nurses assured him that they hadn't been down to pick her up yet. So she should still be here. But where?

His questions died when he heard a door opening. With great relief he walked toward the bathroom where she was just coming from. "Don't scare me like that," he said. "I didn't know where you were."

"And you cared?" Deena asked, staring at him as he approached.

"Of course I cared. I know you want to break out of here but I don't think you're well enough to be traveling by yourself. So here I am to pick you up and carry you home."

Deena walked around him. "No thanks."

"What? Is something wrong, Deena?"

She zipped her bag and turned back to face him. "No. There's absolutely nothing wrong. In fact, I think right here, right now is the first time in months I've thought clearly."

He looked puzzled, she thought, but couldn't muster up enough strength to care. "You wanted us to be over. Your email said so. I've never been in the habit of begging men to be with me. So you can go on about your business."

Max frowned, opened his mouth to speak, then thought better and clamped it shut. He'd forgotten all about the email he'd sent the other night, just before he'd gone into his drunken slumber and before Monica had called to tell him about Deena. All he could think about now was that he had to tell her he'd changed his mind.

"Listen to me, Deena. That was a mistake. It was before Monica called me and I was feeling down and missing you and—"

She held up a hand to stop him. "And it doesn't matter. I can read and I think I can interpret your meaning fairly well. You said we shouldn't see each other anymore, that I should stop trying to fix an unfixable situation because it wasn't worth it. Well, you know what, Max? You're absolutely right. You're not worth it!"

He wanted to reach out to her, to hold her, wrap her in his arms and just hold on. But he knew that wasn't going to work. Deena was angry; that email had changed everything they'd built in the last two days. They loved each other, had admitted it openly and he was actually going to talk to her today about the possibility of her moving to Las Vegas with him. That didn't look like it was going to happen now.

"I was a senior in college when it happened. We were at this end-of-the-semester party, me and a couple guys getting drunk. The party was just letting out and we were a few of the last to leave. As we were walking out the door we could hear a female screaming. So we went back, looked through the house until we found where the noise was coming from. Four guys were attacking her, trying to rape her," Max said the words, a lump forming in his throat. This was part of the reason he'd been so afraid for Deena when he'd heard what happened to her. The memories of how Trisha Linwood had looked sprawled across that bed, her clothes torn, bruises all over her pale body. It had been enough to almost push Max right over the edge. Instead he'd held on to the fact that Deena was safe, she hadn't been raped and she was with him. Or at least she had been.

Looking at her now, Max wondered if confessing everything even mattered. She was so angry, but more hurt. He could tell by the proud set of her shoulders. Yet the dim light in her normally laughing eyes gripped his heart more.

"We didn't think, just started to fight. They'd hurt her so badly all I could think about was hurting them just the same. In the end, there were a total of about twenty guys fighting. After a while I didn't even know who was on which side. When it was all over, I was being rushed to the hospital. Two days later when I awoke and could stay awake and out of pain long enough to talk to the police, one of the doctor's gave me my prognosis. It's called genital tract obstruction. Apparently I suffered a lot of trauma to the genital area. It seemed ironic that because I'd tried to defend a woman's honor, I would never be able to father my own children."

Tears glistened in her eyes but she hadn't moved, hadn't spoken a word.

"It's not an excuse, Deena. I don't have one for the way I've acted. But I know now that I was being foolish. What we have is too precious to let go. You made me see my condition in a whole new light. Your compassionate suggestions of alternative ways to have children made me start to think that having a family might just be possible. I just don't want it to be too late for us."

She inhaled, her fingers shaking at her sides. "*You* see your condition in a whole new light now. *You* don't want it to be too late. This was never just about you, Max. That's the first mistake you made. A relationship consists of two people, working together to make it work. For some reason you thought it only took you. I was never even a player in your mind. Maybe it was my age. Maybe I am the naive scatterbrain my sister calls me. I don't know," she said then took a deep breath. "What I do know now is that I'm sick of it. I don't have to sit on the sidelines waiting and hoping you'll say we can stay together. I don't have to fight for something that only one of us really wants."

"Baby, I do want this," he started.

"No! I won't do this anymore. I so wish you would have trusted me enough with the truth six months ago, it might have made a difference. But not even those unfortunate circumstances or the devastating outcome will make me go back to the state of limbo you want us to live in. I deserve better. You told me that, remember?"

He did remember. He remembered everything she'd said he put her through. She wasn't lying, he'd done all those selfish things and then some. She was absolutely right and he didn't blame her for the stance she was now taking.

But that didn't mean he had to like it.

"Just let me take you home."

"I can get a cab."

"No. I told your parents I'd be taking you home and that's what I'm going to do. After that we can play this any way you want."

She was shaking her head. "I can't...I just can't do this."

Max moved around her, picked up her bag and handed her the purse. "Let's just get you home. Then I promise I'll leave you alone."

Deena looked up at him as if she didn't believe him. She didn't trust him. That look hurt Max more than any injury ever could. But he took it, because he deserved it and so much more.

"I promise I'll leave you alone so you can get better."

He had no idea how he was going to leave her alone for any length of time. But it was time Max stopped thinking about himself. She was hurting, probably physically and emotionally now, and a part of that was his fault. He wouldn't make it worse, no matter how much he needed her right now.

This was no longer about him.

An hour later Max stood at the door to Deena's apartment. She was hesitating he knew, staring at the door like this was her first time here. Or like it was a place she didn't want to be.

"I can take you someplace else if you'd like," he offered taking a tentative step closer to her.

She shook her head. "No. I can do this."

Taking a deep breath she reached into her purse and fished out the keys.

"Let me," he said, holding a hand out in front of her. "I can open the door for you, Deena. That's all I want to do."

With another glance at the door she dropped the keys into his hand and took a step back.

Max unlocked the door, stepped inside before her and looked around. He assumed the place had been a mess, but someone had cleaned it up. Probably her sisters. Turning back to face her he held out a hand.

She looked down at it, then up at him. He could see her struggling with the pain of entering this apartment again and the pain he'd caused her. He hated that look in her eyes. Dropping his hand, he simply stepped to the side and waited for her to enter.

Deena took slow steps, inhaling and exhaling as she did. *One step at a time*, she kept telling herself. She just needed to put one foot in front of the other and she would be inside her apartment. Kevin Langley, however, would not be. It was harder than she'd thought it would be, coming home. Coupled with the turmoil of emotions raging through her about Max she felt like a nervous wreck. But she vowed she wouldn't act like one.

Dropping her purse on the small table near the door

she took another deep breath then looked at him. "I'm fine. You can go now."

He didn't believe her. She could see the hesitation in his eyes. But he only nodded and moved toward the door. She kept her back to him, couldn't afford to look at him again. If she did she would break down, she could feel it. He was breaking her heart and that pain surpassed the bruised ribs, rug burns and concussion.

"I want you to know that I love you, Deena. I've never loved another woman in this world the way I love you. You were the first to break through the barriers I'd so foolishly created. Your smile and lust for life breathed something new inside of me."

Tears burned her eyes, pushed past her closed lids to trail hot paths down her face.

"I know that 'sorry' isn't enough for what I've done. And I know you expect me to simply walk away. But I'm telling you right now that I won't. I love you too much to let you go."

"Max, please," she whispered.

"No. I won't bother you right now. But I won't stop loving you either."

She sobbed, caught herself and tried to breathe through the waves of pain, frustration, irritation. It was too much. She just couldn't handle any more.

"When you lay down to sleep tonight and the next night, know that I love you and that it was fate that brought us together on that island. It took me a while to realize it, but that means something. It means something very special. And I'm not willing to let that go."

The next sound Deena heard was the soft click of

the door closing behind him. Sinking to her knees, she sat there in the foyer of her apartment, arms wrapped around herself, and cried.

Chapter 17

Monica had warned her it was time for her to grow up. Deena reluctantly agreed. Her life was currently a mess, and it was mostly her fault.

She'd met Max and jumped into a relationship with him, a relationship he apparently didn't want. Then she'd turned right around and met Kevin, giving him the impression she wanted something more with him when she really didn't. That had almost ended deadly, or at the very least brutally. It seemed the impulsive nature her family had been complaining about all her life had finally bitten her in the butt.

And admitting it wasn't the easiest thing in the world for her to do. So she'd spent the next week in her apartment, throwing herself into her next writing project and trying like hell to block everything and everyone else in the world out. That wasn't easy. Her mother and her sisters were daily visitors and she knew she'd never be able to stop that. Actually, it wasn't that bad, they kept her fed and even made her laugh a time or two. All except for Monica, who was still her very stern and brutally honest self. In Monica's opinion she was still acting immature, but then Monica was always going to have a complaint. That was just the way she was.

The only person who didn't visit was her father, and she hadn't really expected him. No, that was wrong, she did expect a father to come and check on his child. Even though it was no secret that Deena and Paul Lakefield lived in opposite worlds, he was still her father. But she didn't want to think about that either. She simply wanted to submerse herself into a world she'd created, with characters she could somewhat control.

Either Paul Lakefield had some mind-reading skills to go along with his basic know-it-all attitude or somebody had mentioned that he hadn't seen his daughter in over a week. Because late on a Tuesday afternoon he showed up at Deena's apartment.

"Hi, Dad," Deena said, letting her father in. If it were her mother she would have hugged and kissed her. Even if it had been one of her sisters they would have greeted each other with at least a hug.

Paul Lakefield simply walked in, moving purposefully into the living room.

After closing the door, Deena followed him.

"I wanted to see how you were feeling," he said in his gruff voice.

For a minute Deena just stared at him. He was a good-looking man, Paul Lakefield, even in his late fifties he could be considered attractive. He had a thick build, with broad shoulders and just the barest hint of a stomach beginning to protrude at his belt. He wore a dark suit, white dress shirt and tie, which was his usual attire. Even on weekends he was always in dress slacks and a dress shirt, more proof that his mind was always on business. Deena had his deep mocha complexion, whereas Karena and Monica were on the lighter side like their mother.

"I'm good," she finally answered when she realized he was waiting for her to do so.

"I hear you haven't been out much lately," he spoke as he was taking a seat on her couch.

Deena kept her distance, sitting across from him in an armchair. "No need. I've been pretty busy writing. Besides, the doctor told me to take it easy." Why she always felt the need to explain herself to him she didn't know. Maybe it was because he always questioned everything she did like he'd already weighed the pros and cons and it was definitely a bad idea. Whatever Deena did in this man's eyes was wrong. After a while, she'd stopped caring, or at least she thought she had.

"You should still get out, get some air or something."

She nodded, the only acknowledgment that his words meant something.

"Have you heard from Maxwell?"

Deena swallowed deeply before answering. Her father had never, ever asked her about a man in her life. This was definitely a day of firsts for them.

"Ah, no. We're, um, not really seeing each other anymore."

"Why?"

"Incompatible, I guess."

"You looked pretty compatible to me when I met him in Vegas."

"We weren't really together when you saw us, Dad. He was acting like a jerk and I was just caught up in another mess I'd made for myself." She wasn't exaggerating either, sleeping with Max again had been a definite mistake. Why couldn't she have just let well enough alone? When he wanted the clean break after Hilton Head she should have just given it to him.

Her father shrugged. "It looked to me like he was a man in love. Especially when he came to our room to apologize. Your mother and I both agreed that he might be just what you needed to settle yourself down. I don't think we were wrong."

She stood, really not wanting to have this conversation with her father. "Unfortunately, you were wrong. Max and I are through. There's no future there."

"You sure?"

"I'm positive," she huffed. "Did you come here to see how I was doing or interrogate me about Max?"

"Seems to me they're one and the same."

"No, they're not. I'm fine and Max and I are over. Case closed."

He chuckled.

That's right, her father actually turned up his lips and chuckled at what she'd just said. Deena couldn't do anything but stare at him.

"You were always the feisty one. When you were little you'd argue everything with me, from the logic of Jerry's trappings of Tom on that silly cartoon, to your bedtime. No matter what I said, you argued it."

"You always thought because you were the adult you were right. Sometimes that's not true."

He nodded. "You're right. I'm learning that now."

"Men are always learning stuff when it's too late," she mumbled.

"Is that what you think Maxwell did? That he learned about his mistake and it was too late for you two?"

"He just didn't care enough, that's all."

"Or maybe he cared too much."

She was already huffing.

"No. Wait a minute. Listen to me. For once in your life, just listen to what I have to say."

Deena plopped down on the couch. She folded her arms over her chest then thought that was childish and dropped her hands to her lap.

"Men aren't as easy as women to understand or to predict. Now, the way I see it that boy had a lot of damaged pride. A feisty and persistent woman like you might have pushed that pride to its brink."

"Is that an excuse?"

"No, Deena, it's a fact. This is real life, it's not one of those stories you love to write so much. You can't predict what's going to happen and you can't just pull the strings to what somebody's feeling. You wanted that boy at one time, so much so you waited months for him to call. And now you're ready to let him go."

"Women have pride, too, Dad. I won't keep begging him to be with me."

"From the way he looked at that hospital I don't think you'd have to beg."

"It's just too late. He's gone his way and I have to go mine."

Paul nodded again, letting her words stand. "So what did you learn?"

"What?" she asked, turning to look at him. He'd always asked her that. Every time she did something— from falling off her bike and busting her knee, to trying to sneak out of her bedroom window and breaking her leg. He had the very same question in the end.

"What did you learn from this episode in your life?"

Deena thought about the question seriously. "I learned that impulsivity is a good trait in certain circumstances, but that at some point I need to take my time and think things through before I actually do them."

"You know what I learned, Deena?"

He'd never said that before. "What?"

"That everybody isn't always what I think they are. They don't do what I want them to do or even what I think they should do. Everybody has their own life to lead, their own path to walk. And they'll make mistakes, take a wrong turn, get lost. But it's what they learn during the journey that makes them stronger."

He stood, kissed her on the forehead and moved to the door. "Don't stay cooped up in this apartment much longer or I'll come by and take you out myself."

That stern, no-nonsense voice was what she was used to hearing from her father. Not this understanding and almost compassionate man who'd just sat in her living room giving her advice about her love life.

And hadn't someone else told her that it was about what we learned from our mistakes that mattered?

Sitting in her living room alone, Deena thought of Dalila. She thought of the sprawling estate in South Carolina where she'd spent one fabulous summer. Dalila would have a saying for this, just like she did every other event in life. She'd have some deep introspect and she'd speak it in her funny language and steady tone.

She would probably tell Deena the same thing her father had. Dalila would give her a reason to try again.

Too bad Dalila was miles away.

Deena had walked in the park today and she'd sat at her "spot" writing for about two and a half hours. She'd say she was well on her way to recovery and she'd gotten out of the house before her father made good on his threat to come back and drag her out.

It was a crisp and clear March day, and she'd worn jeans, a T-shirt and a short leather jacket. The sun was shining brightly so she'd slipped on her sunglasses. There was a pep in her step and music in her mind as she hummed her way back to her apartment. She'd just stepped off the elevator when the scent hit her.

Fresh flowers, and a lot of them, the scent was so strong. Heading down the hallway she was more than a little shocked to see what looked like a mini–flower shop in front of her door. Instinctively a smile began to spread as she moved closer. There were roses, all different colors of them, about six dozen. Why the delivery man brought them up here and sat them in the hallway instead of leaving them at the front desk was beyond her. Then again, the part-time front desk attendant, Barry, wouldn't have wanted to bring them all up here, so that was probably why. Just as she was about to become extremely giddy over the flowers her heart stilled, palms going damp. With shaking fingers she plucked one of the cards from the bunch.

If it was from Kevin she was going to totally lose

it. Weeks had passed since the incident with him. And Valentine's Day, she might add, so the arrival of all these flowers was all the more perplexing.

> Pink roses are a sign of admiration. And I
> admire you, for your strength and your
> intelligence, your kind heart and keen
> insight.
> Max

If she were liquid she would have melted into a puddle right then and there. The card was sweet and so were the flowers. She knew that if she opened each one, there would be something equally as sweet and meaningful. But they were from Max.

She didn't know how to handle that.

What she knew for certain was that she couldn't stand in the hallway all afternoon trying to figure it out.

So moving around them, she let herself into the apartment, then carried in all the flowers, arranging them throughout the rooms, collecting all the cards. She was in her bedroom, sitting on the bed with a bottled water when she opened each one. By the time she finished fresh tears blurred her vision.

She was still helplessly in love with that man.

Chapter 18

"What is this?" Adam asked as he walked into Max's office and stood by his desk.

"A butterfly. What's it look like?"

"You want the truth? It looks like a big block of colored glass."

"It's Swarovski crystal."

"Hmm, expensive. You redecorating your office?"

"No," Max answered simply.

Adam was running his finger along one of the butterfly's wings. "Then who's it for?"

He didn't even hesitate. "Deena."

"Oh." Adam took a seat. "Have you talked to her?"

"Not since we were in New York."

"That was over a month ago."

"I know."

"Cole said that Langley pled guilty so there'll be no trial. The judge will just sentence him."

Max felt a bit of relief and just a touch of leftover anger. "To life, I hope."

"Probably not that long but he's definitely getting a personal room at Rikers." Adam waited a beat then said, "Why'd you leave without her?"

Max sat back in his chair and looked his cousin and closest friend in the eye.

"Because that's what she wanted. She asked me to leave her alone and I did."

"So what's this?" Adam pointed to the butterfly.

"I didn't say I'd leave her alone forever."

Adam smiled. "Now you're ready to go after what you want."

"I guess you could say that."

"I'd rather say it took you long enough."

They both laughed. "I agree. It did. But I've had a lot of time to think about exactly what it is I want. I'm hoping Deena did, too."

Adam sobered. "And what if she doesn't want you?"

"Come on, man, I'm a Donovan," he said with a cocky grin.

Adam gave a slight nod. "But for a while there you weren't acting like one."

"I know. The past has always been a dark cloud over my head."

"Sometimes I think you preferred it that way. You were dealt a tough blow, but you survived and you stopped that girl from being raped."

"Yeah, we did. I just felt like I got the short end of the stick. I wanted a family, Adam. Kids of my own like Josiah and Trent's son and Linc's girls. I'll never have that."

"You don't know that, Max. Nothing is a certainty.

There's new medical remedies every day. And there's adoption, surrogates, artificial insemination. You've got options."

"You sound like one of Deena's emails." He'd saved them all, read them over a dozen times, so he knew what each of them said.

"Then she sounds like an intelligent woman. You should try to keep her around."

"I'm trying," Max said, reaching across the desk and picking up the butterfly figurine and staring at it. "I'm trying."

It was midnight in Las Vegas. Three o'clock in the morning in New York. Max pulled his cell phone out of his pocket and hit the speed dial. He waited for three rings and was about to hang up when she answered.

"Hello?"

Her voice was groggy, sleepy, and for a minute he felt guilty for waking her. Then he felt elated to hear her voice at all. It had been a long time.

"I'm taking a moonlit walk and thought you'd like to join me," he said.

"What?" she asked. "Who is… Max?"

"Hi, Deena."

"What are you doing calling me this late? You said you're doing what?"

"I asked you once before if you'd take a moonlit walk with me and you declined. Figured it was time I try again."

She was quiet for a minute and another and Max thought maybe she'd hung up.

"Hello?" he queried.

She cleared her throat. "I'm here."

He breathed a sigh of relief. "So what do you say? You want to take that walk with me?"

"Sure," she said, her voice a touch lower than it had been.

If he were a betting man Max would say she was crying. Not necessarily the desired effect of this phone call, but at least she hadn't hung up.

"So," he began talking as he walked down the street where his apartment building was located. "It's a nice clear night. Lots of stars are out. If I knew any constellations I'd try to show you one. But the moon's there, big and bright."

"I love the moonlight," she said.

"If I could reach up and grab it for you I would."

"Oh, Max." She sighed. "What are you trying to do to me?"

"I'm trying to tell you I love you. And if you still don't want to hear it, I'm showing you. The moonlight is showing you."

"I don't know what to say."

"We could just talk," he suggested.

She sniffed. "About what?"

He turned the corner, walked toward the parking lot where there were a couple of benches and an unfettered view of the desert and, yes, the moon.

"How's your next book coming along?"

They slipped into easy conversation, similar to the nights they'd talked and talked the previous summer in Hilton Head. And when she'd yawned more than once he finally suggested they call it a night.

"It was nice walking with you," he said.

"It was nice walking with you, too."

"We should do it again sometime."

There was a pregnant pause and Max held his breath. "I'd like that."

The walk back to his apartment was with a much lighter step. The smile on his face much brighter.

Progress. He liked the sound of that word.

Early on a Tuesday morning Deena booted up her computer, pausing to rub a hand along the beautiful multicolored butterfly figurine Max had sent her all those weeks ago.

He'd been doing that a lot lately, sending her small gifts. Monica said he was trying to buy his way back into her heart. Karena pointed out that it was something more. Whatever Max sent her had some sort of meaning. The roses in all the different colors, relating each one to the way he felt about her; the butterfly figurine that looked a lot like her tattoo; he'd even sent her books, African-American romance books with passages of declarations of love highlighted. Everything he was doing meant something to her, touched her in a way she'd never imagined being touched.

Her father said he was courting her, something they did in the old days. Her mother agreed and seemed very proud of his efforts.

Deena wasn't really sure how she felt about it. She hadn't seen him in two months. It was early summer now and she thought about him and the time they spent in Hilton Head more frequently.

After their moonlit phone call Max had begun calling her once a day. She'd begun looking forward to each call. Throughout the remaining hours of the day she might receive a text that read, "Thinking of you" or

"Missing You" to which she'd been a little hesitant in replying.

Today, she had an email from him. With a touch of warmth in the pit of her stomach she clicked it open.

One year ago today, I met the woman who would claim my heart, was how the email began.

With each line she read, tears streamed from her eyes. Her heart was full, her vision blurry and all she could do was smile by the time she finished reading. She hadn't responded to any of his emails or text messages before, only spoke to him on the phone. Today, that would change.

Deena hit Reply and watched as an empty box appeared with a blinking cursor for her to begin typing. She put her fingers on the keys, closed her eyes and let the words guide her keystrokes.

One year ago today, I met the hero of every love story in my mind.

Chapter 19

Max's email had ended with this address, so here she was. Deena had no idea what to expect, and truth be told it was probably impulsive and a little bit reckless for her to simply show up. After all, she'd been through so much in the year she'd known Max. But she couldn't ignore that email, couldn't ignore the words he'd selected to let her know how he felt, couldn't ignore the weeks of long talks and openness they'd shared. It was different this time, she assured herself. She knew Max just a little bit better, felt like she understood him more. Most importantly, this time around she felt Max was with her on an entirely different level.

In Hilton Head they'd had the quick and fast rush of passion, the undeniable physical connection that had carried her on an emotional roller coaster in the end. This time, she honestly felt like there was something more substantial between them. She figured she'd find out for sure sooner rather than later.

She showed up.

That was the first thought Max had when he stepped into the lobby of the Ritz-Carlton.

The idea to come to New York hit him a week ago. No, that was a lie. He'd been dying to get back to the East Coast, to see Deena again. But he'd wanted to wait until the timing was perfect, until she'd felt his emotions every day as if he were right there with her. Over the past weeks they'd shared so much. Hell, they'd shared more emotions and pitfalls in this last year than most people did their entire lives together. The fact that they were still in love with each other had to mean something.

Tonight he aimed to find out what.

"You look stunning," he said, coming up behind her.

She jumped a little then turned to face him. "Oh, you're here," she said, a hand with slightly shaking fingers moving from her chest down to her side.

His words didn't seem like enough. She was beyond stunning. In a red knee-length dress that wrapped around her body like a second skin, tying at her side. Her hair was up again, tendrils circling her face. A face that he'd missed more than he could ever explain. Eyes still bright with life and that smile. Everything inside him melted and reformed solid with her smile.

He took a step closer to her, reaching for her hands. When she reached forward as well until their fingers were clasped, Max bent down to kiss her softly on the lips. "Hello," he whispered.

"Hello," she replied.

Ten minutes later they were seated in the hotel's main restaurant, a table tucked in a cozy little corner.

"Your email didn't say you were coming to New York, so I wasn't sure what to expect," she said after they'd ordered and were sitting quietly with their glasses of wine.

"And yet you showed up anyway."

She nodded. "I was hoping," she said quietly.

Max reached across the table to take her hand. "I've wanted to come for a while now."

"You should have."

"No. Today was better, don't you think? It was one year ago today that we met."

"In Dalila's kitchen," she said, laughing.

Max laughed right along with her, letting the memory take him back to those first moments of awareness, the second he knew this woman was going to change his life.

"I've been meaning to ask you, how did everything turn out with Sandy Pines?"

"Just fine. There's a final inspection this week that we'll pass easily. Opening day is July 1 and we're booked through the rest of the summer. As it turns out, Chiniya, you remember her?"

"I do. Juno's daughter."

"Right. She's a marketing major at Clemson. She was just spending the summer working at Sandy Pines. Dalila wrote to me about her graduation in May. Anyway, I figured since she was a native she'd be the best person to work up a campaign that would sell Sandy Pines to tourists. She did a great job."

"That's wonderful. And very intuitive of you to know

she'd work out. You're a very shrewd businessman, Mr. Donovan."

Normally, Max hated when she called him that. Tonight it warmed him. "That's one of the few areas where I trust my instincts."

"I don't know, I think you go with your instincts a lot."

"Let's just say doing that doesn't always pan out the way I expect."

She shrugged. "I guess you could say that's life. You never really know what you're going to get until you get out there and start living it."

"You're absolutely right." He rubbed his thumb over the back of her hand. "There's something else you were right about."

"What's that?"

"You once told me I had options—that we had options."

She didn't pull her hand away but Max felt a shift in her demeanor. She didn't know where this was leading and he wanted to assure her that it was all going to work out. But he didn't know that for sure. All the plans and thoughts going through his mind centered around her and how she would react to the next thing he planned to say.

"I chose the wrong option the first time and the second time," he admitted with a smile, trying to ease her tension. "I'd like another chance."

Deena tried for a smile. "Going for the third strike, huh?"

"No. Taking the final plunge, I hope."

She did pull her hand away this time, sitting back

in her chair to simply stare at him. "You literally live across the country from me. How can this ever work?"

"Did you forget I'm a Donovan? Linc owns a private jet. As long as he and his family aren't using it, I can."

"So are you planning to make weekly trips?"

"Do you want to see me every week?"

She was quiet for a minute. Then she picked up her glass, took a sip. "I'd like to see you every day."

If it wouldn't have caused a commotion Max might have jumped over that table, taken her in his arms and kissed her until she begged for mercy. "I'd like to see you every day, too," he said, still trying to contain the joy of hearing her words.

"But I need for you to know that I want it all. The fairy tale, I mean." She came forward, resting her elbows on the table.

She looked serious so Max cleared his throat as if he were at a business meeting and they were beginning price and point negotiations.

"Happily ever after? Hmm, I think I can manage that," he began. "And if not, I promise I'll do everything in my power to give it to you."

"I want honesty and trust."

Max stood then, going around the table to where she sat. He reached for her hands, bending so that he could kiss the back of each one. "You've got it."

"And moonlit walks," she said, her voice just a little softer than before.

He pulled her up, wrapping his arms around her as she looked up at him. "Lots of moonlit walks."

They were in a restaurant full of people. It didn't matter to Max.

He leaned forward to kiss her.

Deena thought about what she was doing, about what had just exchanged between them. Even though she was not a huge fan of PDAs, she didn't give a damn. This was Max. Her Max.

She kissed him back with every pent-up yearning she'd had for months. Until the waiter came and tapped Max on the shoulder.

"Your dinner is served, sir."

The interruption reminded them of the intercom interruption in the hospital and they both laughed. Sitting down to eat, they chatted lightly over the meal, each of them eager to finish. And eager to begin their new lives together.

The room was fabulous but Deena barely recognized it. All she knew was that she was there and Max was too. That made it perfect.

This was like their first time, but it really wasn't. Still, she felt nervous and anxious all over again. The first thing he did when the door was closed and locked was to lead her to the bed, where he sat, pulling her between his legs. His arms went around her waist and her hands to the back of his head. He buried his face in her midsection, inhaling and exhaling deeply.

Deena rubbed his head, let him take the time he needed because she needed it, too. They'd been separated more than they'd been together, at odds more than at peace.

"I love you, Max," she whispered. "Just the way you are, I love you."

His fingers went to the tie at her waist, his hands pushing the material of her dress apart. She moved her arms and it slid from her shoulders, down to the floor.

He kissed her navel, let his tongue draw lazy circles back and forth. That act caused her to shiver, tendrils of arousal snaking slowly throughout her body.

He pulled her onto his lap, reaching his arms around her to unhook her bra. When that was on the floor as well he cupped each breast, suckling each nipple with slow strokes. Arching her back, Deena gave him full access.

"Perfect. Absolutely perfect," Max whispered against her skin.

Reaching a hand between them, he slipped past the rim of her underwear to separate her tender folds. She inhaled and hissed a breath as one finger slid along her moistness, finding her center then plunging deep inside.

"Mine," he said through clenched teeth. "All mine."

Biting on her lower lip to keep from screaming with pleasure, Deena rode his finger with a fierceness she'd never felt before. He pumped inside her until she was shaking all over, her nails digging into his shoulders.

He lifted her, lay her gently on the bed where he removed her underwear and shoes. Then he stripped off his clothes. She watched with more than passing interest, noting every muscled contour of his body. Bulging biceps, tight pectorals, ripped abs, muscled thighs, long, hard arousal. And he'd called her perfect.

"Max," she called to him, needing to feel him close to her once more.

For seconds Max could only stare at her, at this magnificent blessing he'd almost lost. His lust for her was at full speed every day and every night. But there was so much more. What he felt for her went much deeper. Climbing onto the bed beside her, he touched her, this time with trembling fingers.

"I could have lost you because of my stupidity."

"But you didn't. We're here, now, together. That's all that matters."

"You're all that matters," he said before kissing her. His lips parting hers, his tongue stroking hers, slowly, precisely. She was everything to him and tonight he planned on showing her how serious he was about making them work.

He came over her, spreading her legs with his own. She reached up and twined her arms around his neck. He entered her in one long, slow stroke. She arched, moaned his name.

He pulled out, slow, so torturously slow. Every muscle in his body clenched. Sinking back inside her was like a moment of bliss, pleasure so profound it danced along his spine until his neck tingled. She tightened around him and he breathed in and out, gritting his teeth in an attempt to hold on. "I love you," he moaned.

She wrapped her legs around his waist, locked her ankles and lifted her hips. He was deeper, so deep inside her he felt like they were one and the same.

"I love you," she whispered, swiping her tongue over her lips.

He pulled out, thrust in. "You," he groaned.

She pumped back, sighed. "You."

Release hit both of them at the exact same time, sweeping through the room in a tidal wave of echoed moans. For endless moments he held her close, until he feared he'd crush her. Rolling over, he pulled her with him so that she was half-splayed over his body.

They lay there, perfectly still minute after minute.

"Marry me, Max?" she asked when there wasn't a sound in the room but his heartbeat and hers.

With a finger to her chin, Max tilted her head so that she was staring up at him. "In a heartbeat," he answered and was rewarded with the smile that a year ago he'd claimed as his own.

Chapter 20

July Fourth—Hilton Head, South Carolina

Every room at Sandy Pines was booked, had been for the past four days. There was a flurry of activity it seemed and Dalila was in her element.

It was morning, time had passed for the morning meal but the city people hadn't gotten downstairs until close to nine. She tried not to complain.

At the table was Alma Johnson Donovan, a woman she'd known since she was a little girl. Sitting around her were her two sons and their father. A happier woman Dalila thought she'd never seen.

"I still can't believe you got Beverly and Henry, Linc, Adam, Trent and their families all out here for the grand opening," Alma said.

Max finished off his glass of orange juice knowing

that in a few minutes Dalila would come by and fill it up again. "What do you mean? Of course they'd all want to be here for the opening."

"I heard more people came in last night. It was late but I could hear them on the steps," Everette said, generously buttering his toast.

Ben glanced at Max.

"Well, we should get going into town. We don't have a lot of time for shopping. The festivities are starting promptly at six," Max said.

"What festivities? You haven't even told me what you've planned," Alma complained. "I don't know why it has to be a secret. We're all here now."

Max stood from the table. "Because I want to surprise you," he said, looking over at Dalila, who winked at him. "Now come on, let's get going."

Alma was still complaining but she got up from the table. Everette was taking his toast with him. Ben stood with a nod to Max. And they all filed out of the kitchen.

About ten minutes later, Deena came in with a smile as bright as the morning sunshine. Dalila had to smile right along with her. Today was a happy day.

"Good mornin', Miss Sunshine," Dalila said when Deena came over to give her a hug.

"Mornin', Ms. Dalila."

"You all get a good sleep? Came in mighty late last night," Dalila asked.

"Yes, we did. We missed our flight. Can you believe that?" Deena asked with a conspiratorial grin. Dalila just laughed, her full chest moving with the gesture.

"These your folks?"

"Yes," Deena said, pulling Dalila over to the table where everyone was taking a seat. "This is my mother and father, Noreen and Paul Lakefield. And these are my sisters, Monica and Karena. This is Sam, Karena's fiancé. Everybody, this is Dalila, the best cook and caretaker on the East Coast."

They said their hellos and waited as Dalila fixed them a hearty breakfast. All the while Deena kept checking her watch, Karena kept her gaze off her parents, Monica frowned and Dalila cooked.

Today was going to be a perfect day.

At exactly six o'clock on July Fourth, Broad Creek had been transformed into a billowing white oasis. There was a platform draped with white satin, rows and rows of white chairs tied together with white rope and calla lilies. Huge urns bursting with white orchids occupied both ends of a long aisle covered with a white runner. The quartet hired to sing stood dressed in all-white linen, the pastor and the piano player wore the same.

A long line of people were ushered to the beach by Chiniya and Juno and told to take a seat. There were murmurings and whispers as the Donovans and the Lakefields tried to figure out what was going on.

At ten minutes after six the quartet began to sing Luther Vandross's "Here and Now." Hand in hand, Max and Deena walked down the aisle. They both wore white from head to toe. Deena wore a white sheath dress that hugged her curves yet looked elegant and picture-perfect for a beach wedding. Her hair was pulled up with one beautiful orchid on the right side. Max wore a CK Davis original linen suit with silk tie. The sun shone brightly overhead and the crash of the waves against the shore provided an excellent backdrop.

They read their own vows, both hearing sniffles from behind. The pastor pronounced them man and wife and Max kissed his bride. Then, at 6:34, they turned to face their families for the first time as man and wife.

Photographers snapped photos and the quartet sang again. Max and Deena walked back up the aisle, coming to a stop at the end where Max scooped Deena up in his arms and carried her back to Sandy Pines.

"I cannot believe you married him and didn't tell anybody what you were planning to do," Monica argued the minute she was close enough to Deena.

Karena was standing on the other side of their sister, smiling. "That was the most romantic ceremony I've ever attended."

"Oh, Karena, please. You are so blinded by wedding bliss it's sickening," Monica quipped.

Karena frowned. "And you need some so bad you're starting to get wrinkles."

Monica's hands flew to her eyes. "I am not."

Karena glanced at Deena. "Not there." They both laughed as Monica fumed.

"Look, I don't want to fight," Deena said finally. "I'm extremely happy. I love him so much. I just need for you both, for once, to be happy for me."

"You know I'm happy for you, girl." Karena hugged her little sister tight. "I just can't believe you beat me to the punch."

"I know. It was impulsive. We just decided and then we did it," she was saying just as her parents walked up.

"Just like you always do," Paul said in his stern tone.

Deena really did not feel like this today. And as if she'd silently beckoned him, Max appeared by her side.

"Mr. and Mrs. Lakefield," he said. "I hope you're enjoying the reception."

Noreen smiled. "I'm enjoying everything immensely, Maxwell. This was a beautiful surprise," she said. Then she stepped forward to hug Deena.

"You be happy, my baby," she whispered in her daughter's ear.

"I am, Mama. I am."

When Noreen stepped back they were once again faced with a frowning Paul Lakefield.

He stepped forward and Deena tensed. Max's arm tightened around her shoulders.

"So you're my son-in-law now?" Paul asked Max.

"Yes, sir."

"You finished changing your mind about being with my daughter?"

Max didn't flinch. "Yes, sir."

"I guess that means you love her."

"I do, very much," Max told him.

"Dad," Deena began but Max shook his head to stop her.

"My number one priority is to keep her happy," Max said. "I won't hurt her again."

Paul frowned. "She's my youngest. My baby girl."

It was now Deena's turn to frown. She'd never heard her father refer to her like that before.

"She's had a rough year. I don't want to see her go through that again."

"No, sir. You won't."

"I love her very much, too," Paul said. "I trust that you'll take care of her now."

Max nodded. "I will."

"And you," Paul said turning to her. "You've rushed off and done something big this time."

She swallowed. "Yes, I did." If he was going to yell and berate her she'd stand there and take it. Because she was Mrs. Maxwell Donovan now; nothing or no one could touch her emotionally as long as she had Max by her side.

"I'm proud of you," her father said. "I'm very, very proud of you, Deena Lakefield."

He pulled her into a big hug then and Deena let her arms wrap around him, tears filling her eyes. "It's Deena Donovan now, Daddy. But I'm very proud of you, too."

Paul laughed. Noreen laughed. Soon all of them were laughing, drinking and dancing, celebrating this newest union of love.

"Who's that over there with Monica?" Deena asked Max when they'd finished their first dance.

"Oh, that's Alex Bennett. He's Sam's brother-in-law. I didn't think he'd be able to make it on such short notice. We should go over and speak since he sent you that great doctor when you were in the hospital."

Deena was watching the couple closely. There was something there, a vibe she was getting. "Ah, no. Let's wait a few minutes," she said finally. She wanted to see exactly where this conversation was going with her big sister and the very handsome Mr. Bennett.

"It's a pleasure to see you again," Alex said, coming to stand right in front of her.

He blocked her exit. That was the first thing Monica thought when he approached. The second was, he was so sexy it had to be sinful. But pretty packages often turned ugly when unwrapped.

"Really? And you are?" The question was redundant because they both realized she knew exactly who he was.

He smiled.

And wow, did her heart just skip a beat?

"I'm glad your sister made a full recovery," he said easily. "You make a very attractive maid of honor." He lifted a hand, touched a long tendril of hair that rested on her shoulder.

She shivered. Then straightened her back and pulled away from his touch. "I wasn't in the wedding."

"I'm sure you would have been had they not taken the surprise route. So let's just say I'm offering the compliment anyway."

"I don't need your compliments."

Alex nodded his head, took the glass of champagne she'd been holding in her hand and finished its contents. "That's right, you don't. Doesn't mean I can't give it anyway."

"What do you want from me?" she asked in an exasperated tone.

He stared at her for a long uncomfortable second. "The question should be what you want from yourself. Seems to me you're working really hard to prove a point. I can only assume it's to yourself."

"That wasn't my question."

"Oh, right. It wasn't. So in answer to your question, nothing. I don't want anything from you, Ms. Monica Lakefield."

"Fine. Excuse me." She tried to push past him, but

he caught her arm, pulling her back so that her body was flush against his.

"A piece of advice. Whatever he did, you need to let it go and move on. You're giving him too much credit with this cold, guarded attitude you have."

"You don't know a thing about me," she said through clenched teeth. Her heart was racing now. She wanted—no, needed—to get away from him. Whatever this feeling was whenever she was near him was disturbing and she didn't like it one bit.

"I know you're too beautiful and intelligent a woman to let him beat you."

"Nobody beats me," she said vehemently. "Nobody."

This time she pulled her arm free, wrenching it so hard she knew she'd feel the pain in her shoulder in the morning. But that didn't matter. The only thing she was concerned with was getting the hell away from Alex Bennett once and for all.

At exactly nine o'clock the fireworks began, first spelling out Max and Deena's names then bursting in a spectacular rainbow display.

Max wrapped Deena in his arms and held her tight. "It was a perfect day, Mrs. Donovan."

She snuggled against him. "It was fate, Mr. Donovan."

Epilogue

One Year Later

Pastor Miles smiled at Max then began his usual dedication litany. Sophia Dalila Lakefield-Donovan was being dedicated. To Max's left, Ben and Adam stood as godfathers, while to his right a smiling Deena, along with both her sisters, who were serving as godmothers. Around them were their parents and other family members, and some members of the press were in the back of the church. They'd been at their wedding snapping pictures for their next story. Why it was news that the two families had made a legal union as well as the business one, Max still didn't understand. But as long as Deena didn't mind, he was okay with it.

In his arms was a wiggling baby girl. She weighed eight pounds and three-and-a-half ounces now, at two months old. At birth she'd barely been five pounds. Her biological mother had been a fifteen-year-old street child in Pirata, Brazil, who had showed up on the steps of the Karing for Kidz House in terrible pain and scared out of her mind that she was dying. The young girl hadn't even known she was pregnant. Noreen had called Deena immediately and Deena had hurried to Max's office to ask if they could adopt her.

The question had startled him.

"She has nobody, Max. The mother doesn't want her. Besides, she's too young to know what to do with a baby. She'll be an orphan that our parents will have to find foster parents for if we don't take her. Here, look. I've got a picture my mom emailed to me just before I left the house."

They'd purchased a house in Henderson, Nevada, after their Fourth of July wedding in Hilton Head. Deena was now on her fifth book and loving taking care of the household while Max was away.

He took the picture from her hands even though he wasn't sure his heart could take another surprise. Of course he wanted to adopt the baby. They'd talked about adopting extensively over the past six months. It was an option they both felt comfortable with.

He looked down and everything inside him melted. She was beautiful.

And now, she was his daughter. His little Sophia.

Max looked around, his heart full, as he had the perfect wife, and now together, they had the perfect child. It just didn't get any better than this.

* * * * *

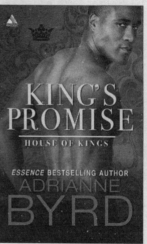

*Their dance
of desire…*

JANICE
SIMS

Dance of
TEMPTATION

Gorgeous, wildly successful sports agent Nicholas isn't
used to waiting in the wings. He's entranced by Belana's
commitment to her craft and her graceful beauty. But how
can he convince the reserved ballet star that they should
share the sweetest dance of all? He's determined to show her
step by passionate step, kiss by irresistible kiss.

It's All About Our Men

KPJS2180711

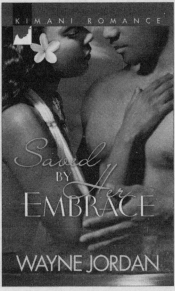

REQUEST YOUR FREE BOOKS!

2 FREE NOVELS
PLUS 2 FREE GIFTS!

KIMANI™
ROMANCE

Love's ultimate destination!

HOPEWELL GENERAL
A PRESCRIPTION FOR PASSION

Book #1
by *New York Times* and *USA TODAY*
bestselling author
BRENDA JACKSON
IN THE DOCTOR'S BED
August 2011

Book #2
by
ANN CHRISTOPHER
THE SURGEON'S SECRET BABY
September 2011

Book #3
by
MAUREEN SMITH
ROMANCING THE M.D.
October 2011

Book #4
by *Essence* bestselling author
JACQUELIN THOMAS
CASE OF DESIRE
November 2011